Broken Lights / 1

Broken Lights

DIANNA HARDY

Illustrated Cover Edition

These paperback covers feature illustrations and/or art by
the author, Dianna Hardy, and are widely available in addition to
the regular genre cover edition. Signed art prints of the covers
may also be available through the author's website.

www.satinsmoke.com

Dedication

This one goes out to all angels.

~*~

Angels watching ever round thee
All through the night.
In thy slumbers close surround thee
. *All through the night.*
They will of all fears disarm thee,
No forebodings should alarm thee,
They will let no peril harm thee
All through the night.

All Through The Night (Ar Hyd y Nos)
Traditional Welsh folksong,
first written by John Ceiriog Hughes (b.1832 – d.1887)

~*~

Broken Lights

Chapter One

"If there was anything we could do to change the circumstances, then of course we would, but as it stands, we need to move forward and up. Especially up. The world has altered so much in the twenty years since you've been here, and the internet has been nothing short of a revolution. Dynamism is the new keyword. Or should I say, 'hashtag'."

Mr Bill Christead – or Mr Craphead, as Norman liked to think of him – laughed out loud at his own joke, tossing his head so far back in his chair that his two mercury fillings could easily be seen.

Norman gripped the black, plastic arms of his office chair, wishing his palms weren't sweaty, and prayed there wouldn't be two wet print marks left behind when he removed them. Like now. He placed his hands on his thighs instead and wiped them on his trousers in what he hoped was a discreet fashion. He could do with not being so shit at this whole confrontation thing, but the reason he worked behind a damn desk was *because* he was awful at the whole confrontation thing.

His heart hammered a mile a minute. "Mr ... erm..." *Craphead, Craphead, Craphead...* "Christead – I'm not sure I understand correctly. I'm proficient at using most aspects of various computer software, as well as the internet, and my knowledge of the company's database is ... well, I was here before it was set up so I know all the—"

"Dynamism, Norman." And then Craphead stared at him as if waiting for him to say something.

Norman blinked, pursed his lips in compliance with the expectation that he *should* say something, although he had no idea what, and then darted his eyes around the large office he'd never made it into despite twenty years of excellent productivity, not a single day in late, with almost no sick days at all. It had never bothered him before. He liked his work safe and constant so he could guarantee an income for his family. If that meant predictable, then so be it. Predictable wasn't a bad word if it put quality food on the table, paid for five star, luxury holidays and gave his two daughters the upbringing they deserved. His wife deserved all the pampering he could afford, too, considering the hours he put in, keeping them apart at times. They'd met in high school. They'd been each other's firsts – first and *only* – and she'd seen him at his worst. She was everything to him.

Norman's eyes landed back on his superior—*what is he? Twenty-five?*—his lips still shaped into the unknown word that never left them. He must have looked as confused as he felt.

Craphead let out a long, heavy, slow sigh. The kind that demonstrated he was talking to an idiot. "You don't have it."

"Oh. Have ... you mean ... er – have what?"

Craphead frowned, but spoke patiently. "Dynamism."

"Oh."

Pause.

Now, Craphead's eyebrows rose as if he'd just had his point proven.

Norman's mouth felt dry, even though his hands were

still clammy. What a strange physiological function that meant water could drain from where you needed it the most – leaving you parched – and travel, instead, to a most inconvenient part of your body.

How dynamic did he have to be behind a desk?

His gaze fell on his feet, encased in polished black shoes, which turned inwards, just a little, towards each other.

"Since the takeover two months ago, we've been asked to make sure all staff are competent in all areas of communication – with people; face to face and all that – essential for a company that will be moving more into the PR side of things. We've also been asked to reduce the number of employees and double up some of the job descriptions. With regards to databases, our new computers can deal with all the inputting and outputting, and ... whatever else is done, after all, they're just numbers. They follow a formula."

Just numbers.

"But someone's got to input all the numbers and commands in the first place," said Norman, his tone rising as if in surprise, but really, he was just trying not to go to where his brain wanted to take him – to that deflating word no one in their forties wanted to hear.

"And you *have* input them, Norman."

Longer pause.

Craphead sighed again. "*Aalll*righty, I've been trying to ease you into this gently, but I'm just going to say it now: we're letting you go."

Redundancy.

He'd known it. He'd turned forty just five days ago. He'd known it was some kind of cursed number for him, because his father had died of a heart attack at the age of forty. 'Forty' had always been stuck in his mind like a leech, draining life, ever since he was eleven years old.

"You'll receive a statutory redundancy payment of course."

Only statutory?

"At twenty full years of service, we've calculated it to be the full amount, I think..." He rummaged through a couple of papers. "Thirteen thousand, nine hundred and twenty pounds."

Under fifteen thousand pounds? Jesus Christ, that didn't cover a year's wage – it barely covered three months! Three months to find another job? Who the fuck was going to hire him at forty?

"So," continued his superior, rising from his chair.

"Oh..." Norman stood. His seat creaked at the loss of his weight.

Craphead held out his hand.

Norman stared at it, blankly. Now? *Holy shit! He means NOW.* "Now?"

Mr Christead regarded him with what was obviously faked sympathy. "Well, yes, Norman – may I call you Norman?"

The first tremor of irritation made itself known. He'd been calling him Norman ever since he'd fucking got here eight weeks ago.

"Your redundancy is to commence immediately. Of course, you can take your time cleaning out your desk."

Oh, thank you very bloody much.

"I'm very sorry."

Say something! Stand your ground, demand to speak to the Board of Directors, refuse to leave, state your case, convince them they need to keep you!

Norman took his hand, numbly. "Thank you."

Pussy.

'Thank you?' Did you really just thank him for making you redundant?

Even Craphead seemed to wince at that as he shook his hand. "Oh, wait..."

His eyes widened, and he felt his breath hitch with hope for just half a second. Another fault of the human condition, 'cause he already knew, logically, there was no hope left with regards to his employment.

"Here." Mr Christead shoved an empty cardboard box towards him that he'd picked up off the floor behind his desk.

Had all this prepared, did you?

Viewing his hand as if it weren't his own, Norman reached out and took the box, and then, like one of those robotic systems that would take his place, he turned and walked out of the room, one foot in front of the other, until, somehow, he'd made it all the way to his desk – the one that had been his work-home for five years. Before that, he'd been at another desk down the hall, and before that, two floors down.

Twenty years.

He'd known his wife for twenty-two.

Still detached, he began to place his belongings into the box, one by one. It should have taken longer. It didn't even take ten minutes.

He looked around at his peers. Most avoided his gaze; some threw him 'I know how you feel' and 'I'm so sorry, but I'm glad it didn't happen to me' looks.

His colleague, Simon, was the one who knew him the best even though he was only twenty-eight – he had been here three years. Those Norman used to work with, way back when he'd started, had all left; sought out new and better positions years ago. Riskier positions.

But Norman had had a baby on the way at the age of twenty-five. He hadn't been willing to risk anything, and it was a decision he'd been happy with. His eldest, Lindsey, was fifteen now, a top student, and about to start her GCSEs at school – a really damn good, independent school.

How the hell are you going to pay for that now?

Simon wasn't in today. He was at a job interview, but Norman was the only one who knew that.

Donning his scarf, coat and gloves to keep the October chill out, he picked up his box and shook away the non-sensical visual of a red carpet rolled across the floor as *My Way* played in his mind on repeat, and walked towards the lift that would take him to the exit.

Six months, he calculated as he pulled into his street. Six months was how long he could afford to keep things going with the money he had in his current account, instant access savings, and his redundancy package.

Even if he were able to go a bit longer, the clincher would come next June when the school fees needed to be paid for the start of the new school year – that would wipe him out. But maybe he'd have found some other form of work by then.

Yes. There are an indefinite number of toilets that need cleaning, my old mate.

Fuck.

He killed the engine right there, where he'd stopped by the side of the road, not wanting to pull into his drive-way for some reason. Maybe shame; maybe guilt. *How could you let this happen to your family?*

He exhaled. Tina would understand – of course she would. She was his rock. It wasn't the first time he'd had problems at work, and although those had been minor – nothing like this – she would help him piece everything back together. They'd get through this, after all, they'd gotten through everything else.

He glanced at his box on the passenger seat, then grabbed his wallet from his pocket and opened it to see the photo in the clear window inside. It was one of their two girls at age twelve and nine, both of them smaller, blonde versions of Tina, taken on holiday three years ago. That had been a good holiday; the often talked about two weeks of sunshine, heat and fun, visiting Disneyworld in Florida. Good job they'd done it already, 'cause it wouldn't be happening again any time soon.

Swallowing all his worry, he grabbed the box, opened his door, and clumsily stumbled out of the driver's side. Placing the box on the roof of the car, he reached in behind his seat to pull out his coat and scarf, and stuck them on the box, not bothering with putting them on since he was thirty steps from home.

One ... two ... three...

He wasn't sure if Tina would be back yet from her part-time job at the opticians. God ... maybe he needed more time to prepare before relaying this kind of bad news.

No. It would be better if she were already home, then he wouldn't have to think about it.

Anxiety swirled in his gut.

Tucking the box under an arm, he got his house key out of his pocket and let himself in. This had been their home for over ten years now – big and wonderful and detached. A four-bedroomed beauty in Richmond, London. As he wiped his feet on the welcome mat, he tried to estimate how much they would save by selling it and downgrading to a three-bed. No way would the girls share a room – they bickered enough as it was.

And it's not like they used the one-hundred-foot garden that much. If they went for a flat, they could get something nearly as spacious in lieu of a garden...

Jesus, Norman, stop thinking of the worst case scenario. You might find another job that pays just as well.

Because everyone was clambering all over each other to hire non-dynamic forty-year-olds.

The muffled sound of something falling came from upstairs.

So, Tina was home after all.

Norman let out a shuddering breath and made his way up, his still-numb brain trying to piece together the start of the conversation, but nothing came to mind.

Stupid, non-dynamic mind.

"Oooooohhhh."

Norman stopped two steps from the top and glanced up. Had she hurt herself when she'd dropped something?

He was just about to shout her name, when someone else got there first. "Tina! God..."

Someone ... else.

Someone else. Someone...

Fixing furniture, or maybe the phone line, or maybe a neighbour, or maybe—

SOMEONE ELSE, NORMAN. SOMEONE ELSE.

But no. That was just ridiculous. In fact, it was so ridiculous he almost laughed. The laugh got caught in his throat when—

"Oh, God! Harder. *Harder.* Fuck me hard."

Yeah, that sounds like Tina, quipped his non-dynamic organ. Except...

'Fuck me hard?' Had Tina *ever* asked him to fuck her hard? Maybe once – many years ago...

So, it's not Tina.

And the human brain was stupid. Or perhaps, it was the heart that revelled in idiocy, because the hopeful illusion that he'd find strangers in his bedroom was what he clung onto as his feet moved of their own accord and led him there.

"Mmmmph ... Mmmmmph ... Uuuuugh..."

It's not Tina. It's not Tina...

He was close enough to hear skin slapping skin now.

It's not Tina. It's not Tina. It's—

"Ooooooooooohh!" Tina's face scrunched up, her button nose wrinkling – this was her orgasm face – as some dick fisted her hair and pummelled into her from behind.

Literally some dick, because Norman couldn't look up from those hips pounding into his wife – the guy's dick was all he saw. A bit of it, anyway, repeatedly, every half a second. Oh – and his buttocks.

Nice.

They were – they were really nice and firm and all clenching as he slammed himself into—

"Holy shit, woman!" cried the dick, and then he slapped her on the arse.

That seemed to be the right thing to do, because Tina's "oooooh" turned into a "yaaaaaah" and she came.

Norman couldn't feel his body.

Norman couldn't move.

But he was clearly capable of function, because his eyes, as if caught by a magnet, were pulled towards the wardrobe mirror, where he could see part of Tina's face from the way she was positioned – the way *they* were positioned – sideways on the bed, and facing away from the door. They wouldn't be able to see him in the reflection, just themselves.

How lovely.

His eyes insisted on travelling upwards against his better judgement – as if he were witnessing a car wreck – and rested on the left half of dick's face which was all he could see of him in the mirror.

Dick was blond, hair hanging to the tops of his shoulders, tanned and well-trimmed. He looked the original surfer dude, minus the surfboard. Where the fuck had Tina found *this* guy?

The question came from very far away, as if every part of Norman, bar his traitorous eyes, were on shut down.

He couldn't feel a goddamned thing.

He knew he should be raging – angry – but there was nothing there. He couldn't even feel the ground beneath his feet, but he *could* see the moment Surfer Dick rode that wave – the very second he climaxed inside his wife.

Something clattered onto the floor, again sounding muffled from some perceived distance.

Norman slowly looked down.

Oh.

He'd dropped his box.

"Oh, god! Oh, SHIT!" If Tina was still orgasming, it was now with a look of pure horror on her face. And this time, Norman could see *all* her face, because she had turned her head and was staring straight at him. She gripped Surfer Dick's thigh, digging her painted red nails in deeply. "Off!"

"UGH!" was his response. He didn't appear to have heard her. He didn't appear to have heard the box fall either, not even breaking his ... thrust. And it really wasn't fair that his thrusting seemed in time with Norman's own heartbeat pounding in his ears, as if what this twat was doing and what he was feeling were somehow fucking connected or something. He *didn't* want to feel *any* connection with this guy.

"OH! *OFF!*" shouted his wife.

"Wha ... babe ... can't ... still coming..."

Well, that was great.

Tina's eyes grew misty as they remained fixed on Norman, her lips trembled, and a "No" escaped her as she brought one arm up off the bed and flung it across her breasts.

That was it – right there. Right fucking *there*.

Norman shook; choked on air as an alien hurt invaded his chest.

It was strange how he'd felt nothing on seeing his wife deep-dicked on their own bed – *their bed* – by some sun-streaked, would-be cover model, but her covering herself up...

His eyes filled with tears that didn't quite fall.

Her covering herself up; shielding her nudity from him – her own husband – was what did him in.

And still, words escaped him, just like in the office when Craphead had offered him his hand.

Are you going to thank her, too?

He didn't know why his inner voice was so snarky – he didn't need the knife to go deeper, it was wedged in about as much as it could be.

"I'm sorry," Tina sobbed, the surfer still in her. "I'm so sorry."

The man finally caught onto the fact that something wasn't right – hallelujah – and turned to see what Tina was looking at.

His eyes became the size of saucers. "Whoa..."

Understatement.

He pulled himself out of his wife, and Norman almost wished he hadn't, 'cause he really didn't need to see or *hear* that, for god's sake.

Nausea whirled in his gut, but it was muted by his still-in-shock state. He noted that the guy was of average size – he didn't own some monster penis that belonged only in porn videos and mags. In fact, Norman might even be a bit bigger. He noted that he had a condom on, and he also noted, with disgust for himself, that he felt relief over that. The last thing he wanted to feel was relief or ... *anything* that suggested this was acceptable in any way. It wasn't.

But when he looked at his wife's face, painted with tears, the first thing he wanted to do was take her in his arms and comfort her.

That was the second thing that did him in: the slowly-sinking realisation he might never hold her again.

He managed to tear his eyes away from the scene as clothes were hurriedly snatched from the floor.

Cotton rustled. His vision swam.

He turned and walked out the bedroom, not knowing how he made it back down the stairs without tripping over and having some fatal accident, and went to the living room instead.

Every sound that greeted him was like a punch to his ribs: footfalls, the low murmur of voices, the man running down the stairs – his steps lighter than Norman's, but heavier than his wife's – the front door opening, the front door closing.

Yesterday's shirt was draped across the back of the sofa. He'd spilled mustard down it, so couldn't wear it today. Tina's fluffy sheep slippers sat by the foot of the same sofa, one of them on its side 'cause it never stayed up of its own accord. Gemma's – his younger daughter's – *One Direction* CD case lay open and empty on the coffee table, a crack down its plastic cover.

He sensed his wife enter the room, but didn't turn – didn't want to see her pained face. *She* was in pain?

The knife twisted.

"Norman?" she whispered.

He finally found his voice, although he didn't know what he was going to say until he'd said it. "This is our home."

More sobbing, and he finally gave up and turned towards her.

"I'm sorry, I'm sorry..."

His ruined heart was fucking useless because it went out to her. *This is fixable...* Jesus Christ, this was their *home.* He didn't want to lose ... *this* – not this. Not her. Not everything they'd spent over two decades building, and surely she didn't either, did she? This was *everything.* Maybe he could forgive her... Maybe he could push past this; it was just a fling – a careless, one-time—

"I met Chad six months ago."

Chad? There were *actually* people called Chad in this country?

Six months, Norman, did you hear that? Six months, pointed out the unreasonably calm part of his mind that had been listening to her more important words. "Six ... months?"

"I ... I needed more," she got out between yet more tears. "I've been trying to tell you for years, Norman, but you didn't hear me – you *haven't* heard me for a long time."

Eh?

"I met him at the opticians. He needed a contact lens check, and new glasses with a bendable frame that stay on while he does all his sports – he's a watersports instructor – and I was measuring him up for his frames and he was just so funny and dynamic, and we had a lot in common, and he reminded me of how I used to love doing sports myself – you know, before the kids and everything – and one thing led to another and—"

Dynamic.

Her voice faded as his head buzzed. She was telling him *Chad's* fucking life story while trying to explain away the whole 'having an affair' thing ... because having an affair was somehow okay ... because *somehow* it was all his fault, because he hadn't *heard* her.

And *Chad* was *dynamic.*

"—vorce, and you know I'd move out except the kids need to be here because of their schooling and—"

"What?" What had she said? How long had he been zoned out? He hadn't heard what he'd thought he'd heard. He hadn't. No. He hadn't...

The silence between them stretched, and she cocked her head to one side, sympathy all over her countenance. "I want a divorce, Norman," she said, quietly.

He didn't know why that statement all but knocked him off his feet considering he'd just caught her in bed with another man, but it did. It wounded him more than walking in on them.

"I really am so sorry you found out like that, but ... it's not a one-time thing, and even if Chad wasn't in the picture, things haven't been okay between us for a long time."

"They haven't?"

She sighed, her crying finished, and ran a hand across her face. "No, Norman, they haven't."

Had he really not heard her? Had he not been listening? How could that be? He knew her inside out ... didn't he?

Is that a rhetorical question, or are you a bigger moron than I thought?

"But ... they can be. I can make it right. I mean ... let me try."

She shook her head.

"I've *just* found out about this. It's been – what? Not even half an hour. Just give me a week or something to—"

"No."

The pause was deafening. "No?"

"No," she repeated with more finality.

"So ... that's it, then? Twenty-two years just—"

"I love you, Norman, because I always have, and a part of me always will ... but I'm not *in* love with you anymore. I haven't been for years, and I can't make myself be."

Losing his job suddenly seemed trivial – he hadn't even told her about that yet – but it didn't matter, because he'd just lost his lover, his friend, his lifeline, his everything. His kids?

God ... please not the kids...

This time, there was no red carpet in his mind; no Frank Sinatra crooning irony at him. There was just a wide, black, infinite chasm which seeped cold into him – a cold that became solid ice when she stared directly at him with blue eyes he knew like the back of his hand, since they were teens, and repeated that agonising word that made 'redundancy' redundant.

"I want a divorce."

Chapter Two

Sleep my child and peace attend thee,
All through the night.
Guardian angels God will send thee,
All through the night.
Soft the drowsy hours are creeping,
Hill and dale in slumber sleeping;
I, my loved ones' watch, am keeping,
All through the night...

The song sounded over the hum of people's voices and in the far recesses of Norman's mind, where he pushed it. The *far* recesses...

Who was singing this version anyway? Some female pop star he wouldn't know the name of, but was sure his daughters would. Welsh is what it was – its origins. His dad used to sing it.

"One second." He attempted a laugh. It came out a burping snort instead. "That's all it takes, you know? And everything changes – everything's just ... gone."

The woman looked at him with what had faded from an almost endearing pity to a silent plea of escape. There was a bit of disgust there too. Life was great.

"I mean ... why would you do that? Why?"

The disgust on her face coupled with annoyance. "Why would I do that? Are you always such a wanker? *I'm* not the one who left you, okay?"

"No," he stuttered out, gripping the edge of the bar with his left hand for balance, "I don't mean *you*. I mean 'you' as in 'women' – females. Why would you do that?"

"Jesus Christ," she mumbled.

Yep – he was, in fact, being 'the wanker'. Turned out, if you found some other guy pulverising the love of your life with his junk, the image kind of stayed stuck there, scarred in your mind, the taint of which seeped into your soul and made you into the loser you never wanted to be.

The short-haired, brunette woman he'd met ten minutes ago, who had had the courtesy to humour all his failures for a short while, was obviously done with that. She fished a small round object from her hand bag, her nose a little wrinkled in disdain, and placed it on the bar in front of him.

"What's this?"

"It's a good-luck-with-the-rest-of-your-life gift – from me to you."

He stared at it, not quite understanding, and then looked at her.

She gave him a tight smile. "It's a mirror."

She turned and walked off, back towards the two friends she was with, both of whom were trying not to look like they were laughing at him behind their hands.

It didn't spear him, though. His previous, nearly-two-month-old wound was still wide open.

He left the 'gift' where it was and brought his glass to his lips.

It was an acrid, sour burn, and had never been his favourite drink, but it was the crude shit you downed to lose yourself, and forty-five days, eight hours and thirty minutes on, he was no closer to finding where the fuck he was supposed to be, how he was supposed to feel, and what the blazing hell he was supposed to do next.

Jack Daniels understood.

Jack could make him forget the 'tick' of the second hand on his watch, and on every bloody clock his eyes landed on.

But it was a pissing shame he was sitting alone in some pub near Whitechapel Tube Station, having been abandoned by his ex-workmates.

Let's go to Liverpool Street, they'd said. Yeah, great, Liverpool Street was nice enough nowadays – it had a vibe and he didn't want to go home to the bedsit he'd rented out in Twickenham last month. It was a dive, but he still couldn't figure out if it was better or worse than the twelve days he'd spent sleeping on his couch, 'cause he hadn't laid a finger on that bed again. Not since...

Yeah. No.

Everything swam as he struggled to breathe, the noise of chatter too sharp for his ears.

"You having another?"

What?

"Last orders."

Was it eleven o'clock already?

"It's nearly midnight."

Ah. He'd asked that out loud.

"Last orders are at midnight here. We jumped on the new extended licence legislation ten years ago."

Norman grunted. Yeah, he had a vague recollection about that being mentioned in the News, but ten years ago, he hadn't gone out drinking – he'd curled up under the duvet with Tina while they talked about their day, and what the girls had been up to, until they'd both fallen asleep.

His chest tightened.

The barman's face fuzzed in and out of focus before Norman managed an intake of oxygen – if one could call it that in here – and nodded once. "Yeah, one more, thanks."

One more. Then he'd fuck off.

The barman looked at him with no sympathy whatsoever, and poured him another Mr Daniels. That was fine. Norman didn't need sympathy. He just needed the crushing hurt to end.

This pub was okay. His ex-colleagues were celebrating Simon finally leaving, now that he'd found a new job, and Simon had been good enough to invite him along. Out of the pleasure of his company, or sympathy, who knew.

They had all decided that for his goodbye pub crawl, it would be a good idea to traipse from Liverpool Street, near work – where he *had* worked – to Whitechapel, and two hours later, Norman had been left here as everyone else, including Simon, had gone their own way.

Whitechapel kind of sucked. It made him think of Jack The Ripper, which in turn made him think of murder and prostitutes, which unfortunately conjured up the image of his wife getting her bum slapped whilst fucked by someone that wasn't him, and he'd damn well slurred that to the barman exactly half an hour ago, to which his reply had been a raised eyebrow and a factual reminder that Whitechapel had also been home to the Kray twins. Oh, and The Elephant Man – he'd died right there in that hospital across the road.

Whores, gangsters, and a deformed man-come-circus freak, victimised by destiny. Such a rich history, this part of town, where all life's beggars found their fate.

That's why you're here, my boy – you fit right in. Did you think you were meant for the high road? Nope. Here's where you belong.

A newly filled glass was put in front of him. Whiskey sometimes looked like stale piss.

He shoved a fiver across the bar, refused to think about that point in the not-so-distant future when all his notes would run out, and let the crude liquid wash over his tongue.

This had better be your last. You still have to get home.

Home.

Right.

That place where the heart is.

He took another swig.

"Fucking jerk!" came the insult from somewhere behind him.

Hoots were thrown into the air as Norman turned in his seat to see what the fuss was.

The barman muttered something intelligible under his breath.

A hard 'smack' sounded as a fat, greasy-looking bloke landed his palm squarely on some girl's arse. She worked here, he seemed to recall. She resembled a ferret, all wild, and small, and pissed off and like she wanted to dart around all over the place.

Or maybe everything just looked like a blur 'cause he was drunk. And what the fuck was it with all the spanking? Why was God torturing him?

"*That's* what I'm talking about," rumbled greasy bloke, hand still on her butt-cheek.

"Oh, yeah? Here's what *I'm* talking about."

The pint of what Norman assumed was his last order, went over his head.

"Jesus-mother-fucking-Christ, Rosa," hissed the barman behind him.

"*Bitch!*" roared the man. He wasn't getting that sticky liquid off him or his clothes without a hot shower and half a bottle of Persil – not that either would help with the suede of his jacket.

She slammed the empty glass on his table and raced away from him back to the bar. Ferret was right – the speed she moved at was pretty unbelievable.

"What the fuck?" steamed the barman, addressing her.

"He's a prick, Dan. He knows Zane – reckons he's got the green light."

"I told you, I don't give a shit about your personal crap. We all have crap. This is work. There's not even half an hour 'til closing – you couldn't keep yourself in check?"

She was fuming, face red, eyes wet. "You *know* what I go back to."

"I told you, I don't—"

"Give a shit. I know." She took in heavy breaths, trying to calm herself down as worry crept into her rage-fuelled blue eyes which were framed with the blackest, thickest mascara. It was a stark contrast to her bleached dread-locks which hung long and heavy past her shoulders; her shoulders and both arms, sleeved in tattoos – all floral – some of the visuals of nature, twisted with images of dark-ness and decay. She was a goddamned secret garden.

Norman found himself fascinated, although he wasn't sure why. Tattoos and dreadlocks were not things he'd ever stopped to admire on any woman, not to mention the stud in her nose and the bar that skewered her small belly-button, just peeking out from under her top.

Looked painful.

She looked pained.

That must be it – he connected with her pain. Or per-haps it was her fury. It tugged at something inside him; his own muted anger he didn't seem able to express. He suddenly felt every bit the non-dynamic person he'd been labelled as. Subconsciously, he tugged at the untucked seam of his shirt and sucked his gut in a bit.

"Fuck, Dan, don't fire me," her voice had dropped low now. "I'm sorry, I just lost it, but you know Zane will lose it worse if you fire me."

"He's the only fucking reason I keep you here."

"Yeah," she clipped out, bitterness audible. "And he reminds me of it often." She glanced back at the table she'd come from, and Norman followed her gaze.

The guy had gone.

He turned back to ... what was her name again?

It was now fear that reflected in the sheen of her eyes on noting that he'd disappeared.

"You shouldn't put up so much of a fight," said Dan, begrudgingly, and then he walked away to deal with a punter leaning over the far side of the bar.

"Right," she muttered to herself, "that's what all the dicks say."

Norman's gaze was pulled to her hands as she dried a glass with a rag of a tea towel. Bleeding roses decorated the insides of both her wrists. *Slit flowers,* he thought, and then he frowned. He couldn't tell if those were faint bruises on her wrists or the colour of the ink...

"What the fuck are you looking at?"

He jumped in his seat, head snapping up, startled, only to see her staring just past his right shoulder. Relief battled with frustration – was he that invisible?

The object of her lashing tongue seemed to bite his own. "I just want my last order."

She exhaled heavily, her shoulders sagging, making every single petal and leaf on her arm wilt, and got on with her work.

The buzz in the pub returned to normal levels now the show was over, and Norman downed the last of his drink.

Right ... home. Or at least, a box-sized bedsit in Twickenham. Tomorrow was Saturday. He wondered if Tina would let him see the girls this weekend. His hours with them hadn't been arranged this time because Gemma had a dance performance at the theatre. The tickets had already been sold out by the time he'd heard about it. Tina had scolded him for it, Gemma had been devastated, and he was pretty sure Lindsey hated him now, but how the fuck was he supposed to know these things if no one told him?

He longed to know how they were – what they'd been up to – and even though he knew he'd miss having them in his life, he never knew exactly how much, or the fierce way that longing would present itself. And now, it was nearly Christmas.

He muffled his groan of internal despair, and made his way to the toilets to relieve his bladder before the long tube ride home.

He decided on a cubical instead of a urinal, shut the door and sat himself down. Quiet time with all his mangled thoughts was preferable to getting walked in on.

It was so bloody hard to think about Tina now, without the thought ending on their bed with ... *that* guy. Shit. He thought about the dreadlocked girl instead. Not girl - woman - although he couldn't pinpoint her age with the way she covered herself in make-up and ink. He wondered about her 'personal shit'. Was it as shitty as his? His mind filled with the flowers on her arms; stems wrapped around snakes and skulls and blood and more intricate things he hadn't had time to decipher. Oddly beautiful images he probably wouldn't find beautiful if he wasn't drunk - or if his world hadn't just ended – but they had been beautiful, with an air of deadliness. Like a warning to keep out.

"Shit," he exclaimed out loud, straightening up on the toilet. Fuck. He'd drifted off? *Shit, shit, shit.* He stood, zipped himself up, and glanced at his watch. He was going to have to hurry to make all the last trains. *Idiot.*

He stumbled out of the stall, even though he tried not to, and made it to the sink, where he washed his hands and splashed cold water on his face to sober himself up. His reflection stared back at him in a slightly haunted fashion. He looked bloody wrecked, but you wouldn't know he was forty. He'd never looked as old as he was. Viewed as the chubby dweeb at school, his voice had broken after everyone else's. He hadn't needed to shave 'til he'd gone to college.

He wasn't as chubby as he'd been at school, and he wasn't fat, but he could do with losing his slight muffin top, although he bloody hated the gym.

His mid-brown hair – now a bit longish, 'cause he hadn't bothered doing anything with it – was usually a normal length, cut in a normal fashion. His blue eyes, shadowed with recent events, were a sort of dull blue-grey – not any kind of interesting blue – and the lower half of his face sported almost two weeks' worth of hair growth.

He tried to imagine himself with tattoos up his arms, or shaggy rock 'n' roll hair, or even the opposite – a grade one crew cut.

He just couldn't see it.

Normal Norman. No wonder Ferret woman didn't notice you – you blend into everything.

When he came back out, the pub was already empty. How long had he been in there? "Hello?"

A head popped up above the bar – that Dan guy. Good

looking, really. Solid, trim body from what Norman could see, not that he was looking.

Yeah, you are.

Yeah, he was. 'Cause since Surfer Dick waltzed into the equation—*thrusted into the equation, more like*—he suddenly couldn't stop judging other men's physiques. It was part of his new low. "Sorry. I was taking a leak and must've—"

"Door's still unlocked. You're fine."

"Thanks." He nodded a goodbye and made his way out of there, not sure why he felt disappointed at the lack of further conversation – it's not like he knew the guy. But he'd eavesdropped on him and the Ferret woman talking and felt he knew him a little better than he had two hours ago.

He's not your friend, Norman, and he'd never be your friend. Guy like that? Guy like you? Nah.

Snarky Norman was back inside his head. Fucking wonderful. He couldn't even drink him into oblivion.

He stopped on the pavement, and while he tried to get his bearings, fumbled in his coat pocket for his Railcard. A handful of receipts, tissues and change came out, a number of coins falling and clattering on the cement – damn loud against the dead of night. Where was all that people-buzz? It seemed no one hung around this area gone midnight. At least, no one was hanging around tonight.

He cursed his clumsiness, grabbing what he could, then proceeded to chase a pound coin that was rolling away faster than he appeared able to think.

It went into an alleyway between some KFC knock-off pulling its shutters down, and a ... he didn't know *what* that shop was opposite it.

"God damn it," he mumbled. Every step took him into

further darkness and he couldn't even see the bloody pound anymore, although he did hear it stop and fall on its side. At least he felt a bit more with it now, the little fiasco sort of snapping him out of his alcohol-induced state.

After straining with his vision, and shuffling from foot to foot for a few seconds, he finally called a loss on the deviant coin and turned to leave; then stopped dead when he heard a shout, a scream, and something that sounded like a bottle breaking.

Cue to leave, cue to leave... And he was about to do just that when—

"Fuck you – no! He's not touching me! He's not *touching* me!"

That was her. That was *her*. He already knew her voice, high-pitched with a bite, just like it had been in the pub.

What followed next was the sound of a hard slap that echoed down the alleyway towards him, then a muffled cry, and his daft feet went forward instead of backwards, because that was *her*, and it was that single image, of bleeding roses on wrists that held faint bruises, his mind chose this moment to conjure up. The image stuck, bold and stark like some SOS signal – strangled flowers among a wild jungle that needed weeding; needed care; hidden gems that with enough light, could bloom into something spectacular.

And he needed to walk away.

This is nothing to do with you.

He stood still, battled with himself, turned back towards the entrance of the alleyway he'd just come from—

"Yes he fucking well is, and he fucking well *will*. What kind of cunt do you think you are? You're *my* cunt, got it? No one's making a living on your shit wages from my fucking useless brother, so if someone wants to pay decent money to have some fun with you, you have some fucking fun!"

Jesus Christ!

Another slap. An erupted sob that to his ears sounded as if she hadn't wanted to let it out.

What the hell was she? A prostitute? Was that her pimp? And that Dan guy was his brother?

The street light from the alleyway's entrance beckoned. *Get the hell out.*

"Shut the fuck up! There – mother-fucking bint. All you have to do is keep still. Jerry?"

Another man's voice sounded, along with some shuffling, although he couldn't make out what was being said – just more failed attempts, from her, to keep from crying. But he'd bet anything 'Jerry' was the greasy bloke from the pub.

Fuck.

He recalled the fear he'd seen in her eyes when she noticed he'd gone.

What if that was Tina down there? Lindsey? Would you be walking away then?

A fire truck sped by on the main road, sirens screaming, the size of the vehicle breaking what little stream of light flooded into the alley, and unwittingly, made the decision for him.

Good god, he was going to die.

He used the noise from the sirens to cover his own footsteps as he went further in towards where he thought they were. The path went around a corner, where a huge skip sat, and he slid himself behind it as blonde dreadlocks came into view.

What the fuck am I doing?

He decided to treat that as a rhetorical question, mainly 'cause he had no answer.

A tall man he hadn't seen before had the woman's arms pinned to the wall she was facing, high above her head. He was holding her in place as the fat, greasy bloke, moved his hands under her top, clearly rubbing her breasts as he rubbed himself up behind her.

He couldn't tell if she was struggling, but she was certainly still sobbing, and Norman felt ill. For a minute, he thought he was going to puke whiskey all over himself, but his spinning head cleared, and his eyes fell on a long piece of wood in the skip, about the size of his arm. Nails stuck out of it in a dangerous fashion.

Greasy bloke grunted loudly. He was pretty much dry-humping her from behind. "Not so mouthy now, are you, bitch. You're gonna be one great fuck. I can't wait to get this cock in your pussy."

Triggers were a funny thing, and this one came out of nowhere, right at that moment: the visual of Tina getting slammed into from behind. Only this time, he was *there*, where he had refused to go for the past two months because it hurt so fucking much. He was there in that bedroom, as if he'd walked in on them again. Reliving it.

Anger went from repressed to expressed in 0.2 seconds.

Perhaps the woman was in sync with him, because she lost it. From sobbing to screaming, she slammed the short heel of her boot into greasy bloke's left foot.

He wailed in agony and dropped to the ground to nurse it. The other guy flung her around with a raging shout and punched her in the face.

She went down.

Norman charged. Only he sort of didn't know he was

doing it – it just happened – no thinking.

His next coherent moment saw greasy bloke groaning on the floor by the skip as he held his head – not his foot – and the tall man on his back, shouting expletives as he tried to pull an embedded plank of wood out of his torso.

Norman's brain finally caught up, telling him he'd gone nutso with the wood; had decked the fat bloke across the head, then swung the plank the other way, nails out, to defend himself against an attack from the other male.

A moan came from the woman, and it knocked him into action.

Fear fast replaced anger. They had to get the fuck out of there.

He went to her and hauled her up to standing. She just about managed it, her hand over her nose and mouth, blood pouring out the gaps between her fingers. Her eyes widened when she saw the tall guy on the floor, also bloody – still screaming and cussing – as he tried to free himself of rusty nails.

"Let's go." Norman tugged her.

"Are you insane?" she hissed at him, but didn't argue, as they both raced down the alleyway. However, in their mad dash, they were going deeper into it, rather than out of it.

"Other way," he panted.

"No. This way bends to the right and leads back onto the main road two blocks down."

He wasn't going to contest that. They'd gone too far now, anyway, to head back the way he'd come. He noticed she was hobbling on her right leg. "You all right?"

"What the fuck do you think?" she snapped.

"ROSA!!!"

His heart leapt.

A small sound of fright left her, and she tried to pick up her pace, but her ankle gave way.

She fell before Norman could catch her.

Scrambling to her side, he grabbed her under an armpit, hauling her up again.

She pushed him away. "He's going to kill you," she said. "You need to get lost. Now. *Run.*"

"Not without you – we're nearly out." Although he didn't actually know if that were true.

"Jesus ... I don't know who the fuck you are or what you're doing here, but you haven't got a clue. He won't kill me, but he *will* kill *you.*"

Not if they reached a public place – the main road. "Just keep going," he replied, forcing that forty-five-day-old anger to drown out his fear. Good job too, because a brain-piercing shot rang out and the huge, wide window of the building beside them shattered, spraying shards of glass across their feet, although most of it seemed to fall into the building itself. A huge abandoned house? Or warehouse?

"*Rosa!* You *bitch!*"

The unexpected gunshot had halted them, and they found themselves rooted to the spot, ears ringing, semi-crouched, as the tall guy aimed the firearm right at Norman.

Everything in him locked up. He would have wet himself if he hadn't already emptied his bladder.

He's got a gun.

Trust his mind to point out the blinking obvious, but he hadn't been expecting that. A knife? Maybe. Not a gun. And looking down the barrel of one, for the first time in his life, was nothing short of terrifying.

"Zane," stuttered Rosa, the left side of her face still

streaked with blood from where he'd hit her, "you need to calm down, baby."

His eyes took in Norman, coldly. Very coldly. There was no sense there. This was the kind of guy that had probably been deranged from a young age, and stayed that way. The kind you couldn't save, even though Rosa was trying. "Baby..."

"You *cheating* bitch," he said, quietly.

How exactly he figured that, Norman had no idea. He hadn't been the one forcing her still as some jerk had his way with her.

"I don't know this guy. Zane ... please..." And Rosa was wrong, because he swung the gun slightly to the left and aimed it at her, not at Norman, and Norman knew Zane was pressing that trigger before the bullet sounded, because, even if this nutter's whole perspective was misguided, he knew exactly what it felt like to be cheated on.

One second passed.

In that one second, one hundred things took place, and ninety-six of them were made up of Norman's life flashing before his eyes, just like so many people said happened when you were about to die.

Funnily enough, and for reasons he might never understand, it was none of those ninety-six things from his past that led to what he did next – not memories of Tina; of Lindsey, or Gemma, or even of his own parents and his childhood... It was some strange, misplaced vision of a potential future – not his, but *hers*: dreadlocks gone, soft, natural-blonde hair in its place (even though he hadn't a clue what her real hair colour was) stopping just above her shoulders, she stood on grass under some blue sky. No mascara, no heavy make-up, just a genuine, kind smile, full of beauty and life – the *good* kind of life – as sunlight shone on her and all her flowers, making the ink on her skin gleam all their colours.

In that one second, that was what he wanted: Life. For her. For her to have that chance. It made no sense, but what did when your entire existence hinged on a moment too fast to blink.

He dove in front of her, left hand open and out like a shield, as if it could somehow stop the bullet, and lifted her off her feet as he took both her and himself flying through the blown-out, gaping window of the building next to them.

The shot sounded.

A fiery pain he wouldn't be able to describe in a million years, exploded from his fingers and ran down his arm, wrenching a scream from his lungs that matched Rosa's own.

He was flung sideways, but gripped Rosa tighter and didn't let go.

Somewhere in his mind, as they fell into blackness, he registered that this was good. This new position meant he was holding her on top of him, not under him as he had been, so she would have his body as a cushion when they—

His back hit something solid, knocking the wind out of him and his scream ended.

Everything ended.

Chapter Three

*T*he light was blinding, as sunlight could be, but it was also broken - split in half by an invisible line.

Blinking hard, he looked down at where he was kneeling to find his wrists tied to the edge of a train track with rope.

Looking across the line, he saw another pair of wrists - dainty, feminine and red with ink - tied in the same fashion to the other side of the rails.

This wasn't good.

Norman's gaze travelled up the multitude of bright and dark shades of her arms to finally land on Rosa's face. She stared back at him, looking just as she had in that strange and sudden vision: make-up free, natural hair, and she exuded a kind of soft innocence that looked out of place with the total devastation he saw in her blue eyes. A far less dull blue than his - a clear, sky blue.

She looked past his right shoulder, to somewhere behind him, just as she had at the pub, and he felt his frustration at that small action reignite, when she asked, "Who's that?"

With slight difficulty due to the ropes around his wrists, he turned.

Tina was bent over in a dress, in the middle of a field, picking flowers. The image played out before him like an old photograph, tainted and stained with time and loss. "That's my wife."

"Why is she in black and white?"

"Because that's how I see her now." And god, that hurt. He turned back to Rosa. "What about you?"

She lifted her eyebrows in surprise. They framed her face wonderfully and gently now the dark pencil lines had gone. "What do you mean?"

His eyes shifted beyond her. "What's that behind you?"

She, too, turned her head.

Time seemed to stand still, and when she turned back, a blood red tear fell from her cheek onto the ties that bound her. "Black."

She wasn't lying. She knelt in darkness on her side of the track where that invisible line split the light in half.

"Why is it all black?" he asked.

"That's how I see everything."

An obvious answer, but it rocked him anyway, and chilled him to the bone. How could that be, when she painted herself in so many bright colours?

The chill settled deeper when a vibration ran through the earth under them.

"What's happening?" she asked.

Oh, god... "It's a train. There's a train coming."

He didn't want to die. No matter how crappy his life in its current state, he didn't want to die. He didn't want it so much, that he was suddenly free and able to move, the ropes undone by his will alone.

He immediately reached forward to unbind her wrists, but was pushed back by that line that split light and dark.

The vibrations grew bigger, and he could hear the train now... "You have to do it. Make the ropes come off."

She didn't move a muscle. Tears of blood streaked her face.

"Rosa!"

"I can't."

"You can!"

"You don't understand..." Her voice grew faint as the approaching train grew louder. "I've always been here. I was born this way."

The horn of the metal beast, almost upon them, filled his being to the brim until he couldn't hear, couldn't think; but he could feel, and her pain became his. He was torn - split in half as surely as the scene they were in. He had to throw himself back from the side of the track. He had to leave her. If he stayed, he would die...

Norman gasped awake, the gasp itself an echo of that debilitating pain threatening to tear him in half.

A small, but firm hand clamped over his mouth; a body leaned into him; a cheek brushed his. "Sssshhh ... I don't know if he's gone."

Events rushed back, although not quite fast enough to numb the throbbing in his left hand and arm. Jesus Christ ... he'd been shot. Had he been shot?

The rest of him ached too - his skull felt bruised, his body battered. They'd fallen ... how far?

He groaned against her palm, but she didn't let up; huddled herself into him instead, and for a brief moment, he took comfort in that - in the miracle he still had a heartbeat and that he could feel hers beat against it, albeit erratically. It capsuled them in their own time, out of reality - out of the critical danger they were in - and calmed him.

A minute passed, maybe more, before she whispered, "You still awake?"

He managed a nod.

She removed her hand from his mouth, but her fingers remained on his face, lightly touching his jaw, perhaps because it was almost pitch black down here. "I think he ran when he heard the police sirens. I couldn't hear the feds above us though – not sure they got out their cars. Zane will be back if they didn't catch him. Did you hear the sirens?"

"No."

"They sounded the same time he fired. We were already racing gravity, though. I think we won."

He smiled, despite himself. She had a sense of humour behind her bite, however bad the timing of it.

Her fingers stroked him, briefly, where his lips curved, and then they were gone. "I stand by my earlier assess-ment: you're insane. Can you move?"

"I don't know yet," his voice sounded hoarse to his ears, "haven't tried. My left arm feels ... I think it might have taken the bullet."

Silence ... and then, "We need light. You're likely bleeding, and you might have landed on glass. Do you have a phone on you?"

"No. I mean, I do, but it went dead a couple of hours back."

"I don't have one either. The one fucking day I leave it at home... I'm going to try and find a light switch."

The thought of her leaving his side almost had him protesting, but he kept his mouth shut, 'cause she was right, they needed light, and he didn't want to appear a complete wuss. The loss of her body heat added a new kind of ache though. He wondered if she actually *had* landed on him. And *what* had they landed on?

He felt beneath him with the fingers of his right hand – that arm seemed all right – and found a slightly silky, springy texture. A mattress? Surely not. That would be like the biggest cliché in the world, but whatever it was, they'd landed on something that wasn't hard, cold stone, and for that he was grateful, or he might well be dead. If his survival turned out to be clichéd, he'd pay homage to every fucking cliché from around the world once they got out of here.

He experimented with movement, flexing whatever muscles he could and testing the pain. His shoulders bunched, and he winced, but a few more twitches around his shoulder blades had them loosening up a bit. He tried to move his fingers on his left hand and almost screamed at the agony.

Something clattered a few metres to his left. Rosa cursed.

"Are you all right?" That came out much more sharply than he'd intended, but he didn't want to end up alone down here because she'd gone and done herself damage.

"Yeah. Some kind of tin bucket or something. Wait ... you haven't got a lighter in one of your pockets have you?"

"No. Sorry." He felt useless. *No change there, then.*

"Okay ... I think I've found the wall. Feels like brick. I'm just going to move along it..."

"You didn't get hurt? When we fell?"

"Fell? You kamikazed us through the damn window."

They both became quiet, the heels of Rosa's boots the only thing making any noise; occasionally there was a scuffle of something as she worked her way along the wall in the dark. He was grateful for the small sounds – he needed to hear her. Terror hadn't quite left him, and although he reasoned that his ability to feel pain held a better prognosis than not being able to feel anything at all, he didn't know what state he was in. He was pretty sure he could smell blood, but he wasn't positive, because the continuous, burning, stabbing sensation running up his arm pretty much drowned out all his other senses.

"I'd be dead if you hadn't," came her voice, all of a sudden, a shade softer than before. "Why did you do it?"

"Do what?"

"You know what."

"I don't know – why, I mean. It was a split-second decision – do something, or do nothing." He didn't tell her about his bloody weird vision. It's not like he went around having visions – that was the first one ever, and he didn't even know if 'vision' was the correct term. It was a 'thing' his slightly drunk mind had materialised when faced with its final destination, with nowhere left to go. So, more likely, it had been a delusion. Kinda fucked up – risking your life for a delusion. If he survived, maybe he'd write a book about it and send it in to Oprah.

The silence ensued as she continued on her journey around the edge of the room, until he needed more conversation to take his attention away from his arm. "Do you know what building we're in? Or how far we fell?"

"No to the building – kinda looked like a big, abandoned, turn-of-last-century warehouse to me. I've walked down this way before, but never really paid it much mind. Half of it's boarded up and has been ever since I can remember. I think we fell a couple of floors. Lots of the old buildings around here have underground cellars and things. I think this one might have been used by the hospital once for something or other. When I was little, one of the neighbourhood kids loved to spook us all, saying they used it as an extra ward, and all the loons and freaks were kept here."

He thought of The Elephant Man.

That added a whole new creep factor to their current situation.

And that's such comfy bedding you landed on.

Holy fuck!

"Everyone knew he was lying though. Oh, here ... I think ... hang on..."

With a loud buzz, flickering light filled the room and pierced his eyes, making them throb in time to his injured arm. He squeezed them shut.

"Wow," her voice was hushed. "Maybe he wasn't lying after all."

With his breath held, he slowly peeked out through his lids.

Oooookay. It was important he didn't think about freak shows *or* psychopathic doctors that liked to gut prostitutes. "Jesus fucking Christ."

"Yeah," she breathed out, the cold, early December air forming a soft mist around her words, just as it had his.

'Haunted, abandoned infirmary' pretty much covered it, and he hoped to god it *wasn't* haunted. "Do you think this was really a hospital, or some wealthy person's huge basement which was used as one?" It didn't look *exactly* as a hospital ward might look, but all the right props and tools were scattered around, and bed pans, sheets (yep, that was a lovely stained mattress he'd landed on, and not just one, but four or five, as if whoever had been last out the building decided they needed to be thrown to one side), a couple of bed frames, a metal trolley on wheels... But everything was dated, although not quite turn-of-last-century ... maybe the 1950s?

"Your guess is as good as mine. Look." Her heels clacked three paces, and she leaned over one of the trolleys to pick up a cracked, eyeless porcelain doll from one of the shelves by the wall. Strings protruded from its arms and legs, all of them leading to a wooden cross that controlled the puppet.

He groaned as a rush of nausea hit him.

Rosa placed the doll back and was suddenly by his side again. "Let's see the damage."

That was one way to put it.

He didn't know if he wanted to look, but he turned his head and glanced down at his left hand anyway.

Bloody. Hell. "Oh, shit." He could barely *see* the hand – there was just blood.

"It might not be as bad as it looks."

"It looks pretty bad."

"Blood always looks like there's more of it than there is. I mean, one little cut can look like a small stream. And you've been drinking, right? So your blood will be thinner making it run more easily."

How the hell did she know all this?

He took in her face beneath the painfully fluorescent bulbs. Her skin was so pale under them she looked almost vampiric, and it was starkly contrasted by the ugly swell on her face where that dickhead had hit her. *That's how she knows.*

Some of the blood had come off around her bruise – probably onto his shirt. "You should take care of that," he nodded at her cheek.

She waited a beat before glancing up at him quickly, then back down again at his hand. "This is nothing. Yours might be a bullet wound. I need to find some water – get it cleaned up."

"Wait, no. We need to find the way out. We don't need water, we just need to call an ambulance."

"Can you see a phone?"

No, he couldn't.

She got up and went straight for one of only two doors in the room – the one that looked like the way out.

Norman almost shouted, *No!* Fuck if his head wasn't filled with every scene from every horror film he'd ever seen, telling him nothing good was behind that door.

It didn't matter anyway. When she went to open it, it wouldn't budge.

"It's locked."

"Are you sure?"

More tugging and pushing and pulling... "Yeah."

"Why would anyone lock it from the outside?" He wished he hadn't asked that.

"I don't know, and I don't think I wanna know. Unless we can bash this down, looks like the only way out is the way we came in."

He looked up towards the windowless frame, as she tried the other door – a bit smaller, with slats half way down it for ventilation. "Storage cupboard," she murmured, before closing it again.

God ... they *had* fallen far. Two floors looked about right. Or maybe one really huge one with a bloody high ceiling. *Rotting ceiling.* No way were they going out that way. "We could shout 'til someone hears us."

"No!" she snapped.

He startled in surprise.

Her eyes were lit with fear. "What if Zane's the one that hears? The lights are bad enough, but I'm positive there's no way he'd have stayed put with the sirens, and we need the lights. He won't be able to see them unless directly above us, but he'd hear us calling all the way down the alleyway, which looked pretty much deserted to me. No shouting unless we know he's not there."

Damn. That hadn't occurred to him. And he hated the way her voice sounded on the edge of panic. "We should turn the lights back off." He wanted her calm, and it's not like he could fight back or do shit in this condition if that maniac decided to come down here. He didn't fancy another bullet.

She didn't reply right away, but dropped her gaze and got herself in check. When she looked back up, some of her steel was back. He wondered once more at her age. She looked so young – early twenties, maybe. "Your arm first. Do you hurt anywhere else?"

"No. Just from the left hand up to the elbow – it's not too bad around the shoulder."

"Okay. Well, I can't see anything with all the blood, so ... the lights work." She attempted a smile. "What's the bet there might be running water, too?"

He grimaced. "What's the bet if there is, it'll have been at least five decades encased in pipes. Who pays for the electricity anyway, if it's abandoned?"

She let her eyes wander. "Dunno. But you hear of it sometimes, don't you – rich folk inheriting property, and they've got so much money it, like, comes out their trust or something and they don't even care they're paying the bills. I heard about some French lady once – I think it was in the paper or something – that evacuated her flat during the Second World War, but never sold it or rented it out. Everything just stayed inside as she'd left it, like a time capsule, 'til a few years back when a relative of hers inherited it. She'd been paying the rent on it and everything."

The more quickly and often she talked, the more he heard her East End accent shine through. It was strangely comforting in this carcass of a building – a spark of life, among the dead. He unwittingly shivered, and didn't feel like he wanted to be lying down anymore. "Think you can help me up?"

"Not if it might rupture something. Stay put. I'll find water."

He sighed.

"What was that for?"

"What?"

"The sigh."

"I just hate feeling useless."

She fell silent, for ages it seemed, until he attempted to lift his head to see her.

She stood there, just staring at him in puzzlement. "What's your name?"

"Norman."

"Norman? Didn't know anyone was called Norman anymore."

"Didn't know anyone was called Zane, ever."

She smiled.

It only lasted a couple of seconds, but it was real, it was humane, and that goddamned hallucination that had gotten him into this crap in the first place replayed in his mind.

"It's his nickname."

"Ah." He winced as his head fell back, unable to stay up any longer, but that curious satisfaction at her small smile still warmed him, as if she didn't smile often ... as if it mattered one iota that he'd managed to work one out of her. What the blazing fuck was wrong with him?

He was dying, that was what. *You're dying, and doing and thinking strange things – it's part of the hallucination.*

Maybe there was still a chance this was all a bad dream.

Everything went quiet for a while as she headed for the rectangular sink units on the far side of the ... whatever the hell this place was.

Norman listened as she swivelled the first tap, to no avail; the second to no avail. On the next sink, one of the taps, when turned, produced a sort of chug-chug noise.

She shut it off, and then turned it on again to more of the same. Leaving it on, she reached for the one next to it, swivelled it and—

"EEEEEEeeee!" she shrieked, jumping backwards and clamping her hand over her mouth, eyes darting upwards towards the way they'd come in. "Uuuuuurrgh," she sounded, more quietly, "it's *freezing*. And kinda brown, but I think it might run clear in a minute."

It was better than nothing, although he wasn't looking forward to having his hand examined.

Nothing but gravelly-sounding, running water filled the room for about a minute. He almost didn't hear her say what she said next.

"Norman."

His name on her tongue sounded as if she was testing it out – some alien word she couldn't quite get the meaning of. But it rang sharply through his body; again, warming him strangely and reminding him he was still alive.

He turned his head back towards her, but she was leaning over the sink with a bedpan—*Oh, yuck! That had better be clean!*—filling it up, showing no indication she'd said anything at all.

Now you're hearing things.

He fought off the panic. He hadn't just drifted in and out of consciousness, had he? He remembered as a kid, he'd often hear voices calling his name when he was surfacing from sleep. As an adult, he'd heard it was a common thing, but it had freaked him out when young; had him thinking his dad had been trying to speak to him from beyond the grave. He hadn't told a soul about it, not even his mum.

The sound of running water stopped, and the new silence that took its place left him hollow.

Talk to me again, he pleaded Rosa, silently.

She lifted the bedpan full of water and carefully made her way back to him without saying a word.

The hollow feeling grew into a seeping cold, where the out-of-place warmth of her smile had been. He couldn't shake the feeling he wasn't going to make it out of here.

Chapter Four

"Norman."

She hadn't meant to say his name – sorta slipped out, the way her stupid temper had tonight with Zane's 'acquaintance'.

But he'd been lying there so still, and the running water had sounded so bloody loud, making her jittery. She didn't like noise. Noise inevitably meant something bad was about to happen. Noise was shouting and fighting, and dogs barking and shit hitting the fan. And who the ever-loving fuck *was* this guy?

She turned back to the sink before he caught her staring at him.

He'd been at the pub, she remembered that much. He'd caught her eye because he'd looked so out of place – not one of the regulars – but also because, unusually for her (with *any* man), she'd found him attractive, and that was a big no-no. If Zane had been anywhere there, watching her, after what had gone down with his friend, he'd hunt this guy down if he caught her staring at him. So, she'd kept her eyes firmly off him. Avoided him completely.

And then he went and showed up in the alleyway.

He's the police, she'd concluded. Undercover even, meaning she might end up in just as much shit as Zane. The police were fucking useless. They'd done nothing for her. The one time she'd gone to them, over three years ago now, had seen her back in Zane's arms and under his fists. The beating she'd suffered for attempting to escape the life she'd been shoved into had ensured she never went to the police again.

But this guy wasn't the police – there'd been something off about that assessment. He hadn't pulled out a baton, or a gun, like London police could carry nowadays, or anything. He hadn't talked like them. He'd gone bat-shit-crazy with a plank and no plan, and *then*... That Schwarzenegger stuff with the window? What the fuck? She hadn't seen that coming – she hadn't seen *him* coming.

Trying not to spill the water, she finally made it back to his side and slowly knelt down, placing the bedpan on the floor along with a towel she'd found under the sink, a pair of scissors, a bar of soap, something she hoped was bandages, and a thick pad of cotton, still in its wrapping. According to the packaging, this was a sponge. It didn't look like a sponge, but it would do for cleaning blood. Good fucking job this place had been left with a few supplies. She wondered why it had been abandoned.

"We need to get your coat off."

He groaned, and she almost wished she hadn't stated the obvious, but nothing was going to get cleaned up otherwise.

He opened his eyes and looked at her.

Her stomach fluttered, although she didn't know why. *Nerves...*

It was going to hurt getting that coat off, and she didn't want to hurt him.

He had blue eyes.

And why the hell did that matter?

Because he looks so different from Zane, replied a small voice in her head. This was true, although it seemed so stupid to think it. It's not like Zane was the only guy she knew – she knew loads – but Zane had been such a force in her life for so long, he may as well be all she knew.

She'd virtually been born on the streets, and like all born on the streets, she'd stayed on the streets. A dash of luck had come through for her mum when she'd been around six, and the streets had become Council Housing. But outside of warmth and shelter, that hadn't made anything better, because her mother still knew all the worst people, and didn't know how to leave them behind. Something Rosa could, unfortunately, relate to.

Through a dumb moment of hope she'd never repeat again, she thought she'd seen a silver lining three years ago. She'd thought she could escape her mother's fate, and her own.

Escaping Zane, however, was like trying to escape from history – you never could. History had already happened, and the occurrences that took place in it, paved permanent roads in the map you had to follow.

Zane had startling blue eyes, that were cold and hard, with a streak of madness.

Norman's eyes were soft and steady. Everything about him seemed soft, actually – and warm – and she knew this because she'd landed on him. She hadn't had a choice – he'd been clutching her so tightly, she couldn't have gone anywhere else.

When her senses had returned after they'd landed down here, the first thing she'd noticed in the pitch black was the softness of his body, because it was nothing like Zane's. Zane was hard, wiry – all sinewy, knotted muscles. Having sex with Zane was like having sex with a metal bar, and as suffocating as any prison, and she could do without the sex comparison right now. Honestly, what was wrong with her?

Zane is what's wrong with you; your whole life is what's wrong with you...

To think this guy – Norman – had seen what Zane was doing to her.

She felt her cheeks heat and hoped it wasn't noticeable under these god-awful lights. *Probably not noticeable under the bruising ... no one ever sees anything under the bruising...*

"I'm cold. I'll bet that water's colder. I'm going to bloody freeze."

"I'll be as quick as I can. Maybe just take the one sleeve off – keep your coat on the other half of you. I'm gonna come help you sit up."

She made her way to his right side, lay down next to him, and propped as much of herself, as best as she could, behind his right arm and back. "Say if it hurts too much, okay?"

"It's going to hurt too much," he muttered, seeming resigned. "Do it anyway."

Using his right arm as a lever, and her body as support, they managed to get him upright. She wondered if he was biting his tongue – he was certainly shaking all over. "Norman?"

"All right." He didn't *sound* all right. "Fuck..."

"What, er ... what should I—"

"Get the coat off now, before I change my mind."

Shit.

She raced around to his left, hating the way his voice was so strained. "I need you to lift your arm up."

He winced. "I don't know if I can. You'll have to hold it up, or get something to prop it up with."

Nothing was going to balance properly on these mattresses.

Without really thinking about it, Rosa scrambled between his legs until she was chest to chest with him, and reached under his coat for the arm that lay inside the sleeve. When she had it, she held it firm and stood, taking the arm with her.

Norman stifled a scream, and it was only then that she realised his head was now against her crotch. She pulled a face. Kinda awkward, but there was nothing for it – practicality outweighed awkwardness.

Leaning forward, she grabbed the cuff of his sleeve, stepped forward and pulled.

This time, Norman did scream, and so did she – almost – when his right hand gripped the back of her leg tightly, making her teeter.

The sleeve came off and she caught herself from falling, silently praying Zane was nowhere near the vicinity.

Her saviour buried his head between her thighs, his frame heaved twice, and she distinctly had the impression he was trying to keep from sobbing.

"I'm sorry. It's done – it's off now."

He nodded.

Sudden warmth rushed through her – the same warmth she'd felt when looking at him lying there. Pushing it away, she stepped back and knelt down again.

He had his eyes closed, and she had to resist the instinct to touch his face. She wanted him *with* her – conscious. *Don't pass out.* "I'm going to roll up your shirt sleeve and look, okay?"

He nodded again, but kept his eyes shut.

Getting his shirt sleeve up was easier than she'd thought it would be. All the blood seemed to be centred on his hand, and not on his arm, so the sleeve was dry and didn't stick to his skin. "See? I don't think it's as bad as it looks."

His eyes stayed closed.

It bothered her. She wanted to see the softness; to know she hadn't ruined it. "I need to take your watch off."

He said nothing, so she did, and placed it on the floor by her feet. "I'm bringing the towel and bedpan over now, and I'm going to wipe the blood off your hand. It'll be cold."

This time he grunted, but didn't protest.

She held the sponge between her teeth as she laid the towel under his hand, placed the bedpan of water on top of it, and then got to work.

He hissed when the water made contact with his skin, but she didn't slow down or stop, wanting all the blood gone so she could see the wound.

Red washed away; gold surfaced. A wedding band glinted at her, and for a second she stalled. Her throat constricted as a baffling ... disappointment? ... rose.

Shaking herself out of her ridiculous reaction, she resumed cleaning him up. "There's bruising around your whole hand, and it looks like the blood is coming from under your wedding ring." Her throat constricted around those two words. She swallowed to loosen it. *What's he doing out here drinking on his own, at this time of night, if he's got a wife?*

His eyes finally opened, he looked at her, his expression unreadable, and then looked at his hand.

"See? Here? And there's a dent in the ring. I think, maybe, the bullet hit your ring, snapped your finger back – look at the swelling – and pretty much fractured it, and probably the bones in your whole hand. I can't believe the force of it didn't take your finger clean off. It would have if it had been your finger the bullet hit instead of the ring."

He looked dumbfounded. "You think that's what happened?"

"Well..." she shrugged, "I dunno. But it's as good a guess as any. Explains the dent, the blood – from where the ring cut into you – and the fact that there's no other open wound. I hate to say it, but we should get the ring off if we can, because you're probably going to swell up more around it."

And now he looked pale. *Really* pale. "Or maybe ... it might be okay if we leave it on – I mean—"

"Mmmmnnn." He shook his head forcefully as he let out that moan. "It's ... it should come off. Let's try get it off."

She hesitated, reaching to understand what it was he wasn't saying, because there was definitely something...

"It's okay," he nodded, and then met her gaze.

There. She could fall into the softness of those eyes the same way she'd fallen onto him. They eased her.

Somewhere in her mind, some small voice expressed the opinion that that wasn't a good thing. The voice was too small to matter right now – their survival was more pressing.

She offered him a small smile, and his eyes seemed to smile back just a little. "Okay," she replied, and then went to work.

With the soap she'd found, she cleaned his hand and concentrated on getting the slipperiness under his ring. It wasn't easy. The bruising all over his digits and knuckles was immense, and she had no doubt that every tug and twist she delivered to his broken bones sent a bolt of agony through him, but he gritted his teeth, kept heaving his breaths in and out, and held it together.

The process was slow, and at one point she thought he'd had enough and that she wasn't going to get the ring off, when it began to slip down, millimetre by torturous millimetre. She praised the icy water for keeping his swelling to a minimum.

The ring slid past the thickest part of his finger and she didn't tell him she was going to yank it off the rest of the way, she just did it.

He wailed, she bit her lip in apology, and the dull 'clunk' of the band hitting the bottom of the now red water in the bedpan, confirmed its fate.

~*~

He was pretty sure he was drifting in and out of consciousness while sitting up, but he didn't want her to know that.

The mention of his ring snapped him awake and to attention. It made sense – sort of – what she was saying about how the bullet had dented the ring and ricochetted off it, breaking pretty much all the small bones in his hand in the process. He'd been the idiot that had held his hand up, but if he hadn't, he wondered if the bullet would be buried in his skull. Or hers.

It was kind of a 'wow' moment – a bit of an epiphany – but the brutal pain outweighed all the 'wow' and he just wanted the damn ring off now. Off, so he wouldn't have to think about it anymore.

She was an angel. Maybe a fallen one covered in war paint, but an angel nonetheless ... the way she determinedly took care of him.

Maybe it was to save herself, but that was fine. Somewhere inside him, he knew she needed to do that.

There he went drifting again.

He wanted to lie back.

There was a dull clatter, and he registered that the ring was off his finger. Lightness filled him. Yeah ... it was a bit like flying ... if he could just ... fall ... back...

He groaned in protest when he was jerked forward by the lapels of his shirt. "Hey – wake up."

It wasn't the command, but her voice, edged with terror, that had him forcing his eyes open. "S'okay."

She didn't look convinced, and he wanted to wipe the fear off her face. He wondered if she'd always been afraid. What would that be like? To spend your whole life afraid?

Focus!

Right. "It's okay," he said again, blinking fast to clear his head. "Thank you."

"Stay with me."

"I'm right here."

"It might not be as bad as we thought, but you still lost some blood, and there's alcohol in your system, so you need to try harder to stay awake. I'm going to bandage your hand up, and then I need to check your back for glass."

Glass. Damn. He'd forgotten about the glass.

She did exactly as she said she would do, winding some kind of thin cotton around him, starting at his wrist. He really hoped it was sterile. She ended up twining it around his palm and knuckles, making sure it was wound, tight and smooth, between his thumb and fingers. She stopped before the tips of his fingers, and how exactly she managed to put a knot in the thing was beyond him, but she did. *Not the first time she's done this,* said his head. That thought made him ache, although he didn't know why –

she was bad news and he didn't know her from Adam. When this was over, she'd be gone, back to her life where she belonged.

No. She doesn't belong there.

The ache grew, but his lapse in full consciousness dimmed it.

"Wake up," she snapped.

He did. "Sorry."

"Talk to me. Does it still hurt?"

"Uh ... yeah, but my hand's starting to go numb from the cold, so there's not as much pain ... I guess that's good?"

She frowned. "We'll get you warmed up again soon. Right. Let me see your back – you don't have to move. Just stay there."

Not a problem. He wasn't going anywhere.

With relief, he finally rested his patched-up hand on his thigh.

He felt his shirt being lifted beneath the half of his coat that dangled off him, and then her hands – as icy cold as the water they'd been in – moved over his skin.

He jumped.

"Sorry."

"It's fine." He just felt bad her hands were that cold.

After a minute of what felt like a full inspection of his back and shirt, she moved away and pulled his clothes back into position. "No glass." She reached around him and picked up the towel she'd used to dry and clean him. "I'm just going to rub the mattresses down in case there are shards, but it looks like most of the glass fell on the floor just beyond them."

He said nothing as she got on with her task.

"I was thinking," she looked at him quickly, then back

at what she was doing, "we should move one of the mattresses away from the under the window so we can't be seen and turn the lights off, then hole up in here 'til morning. If it's dark, and there's no light, I don't think Zane will come down here. If he thinks we're dead, he'll keep a low profile. You're not bleeding anymore, but you need rest, and come six in the morning, there'll be people outside going to work – the nearby shops will be stocking up – we can holler for someone then. Six is only ... maybe five hours away? That's not long."

"Sounds good." And it did. He was about to collapse from exhaustion. Even the possibility they might still be in danger wouldn't keep him awake, he was sure. Five hours flew by when you slept.

"Here."

He glanced up at her, aware that he'd zoned out again.

She stood in front of him with his coat sleeve out. "Let's get you warm again."

This time, when he raised his arm, there was much less pain – whether from the numbing cold, or because of her care, he wasn't sure – and he found himself able to move the limb on his own.

Carefully, he aimed his hand into the sleeve and she slid it on.

"You worked wonders. Thank you."

The silence grew heavy.

Had he said something wrong?

He caught her staring at him, and although he couldn't figure out what she was thinking, or how he might have put his foot in it, she didn't look away this time.

"I hope your wife thinks so, too. She's gonna hate me a whole lot for getting you into this mess."

Odd. He hadn't even thought about Tina's possible re-action; not even when the ring had come off. "I'm not sure she'd care. Well, maybe she would ... but I'm not sure she's got the right to an input about it."

"What do you mean?"

His chest tightened. Did he want to say it out loud? He found his gaze drawn to the bruise on her cheek; her nose and upper lip swollen; a small amount of blood crusted around her nostril ... and found that he did. "I walked in on her, with someone else, in our bedroom."

"Oh."

"Mid-orgasm."

Her dark, pencilled eyebrows hit the ceiling. "Shit."

"Yeah."

"Well, fuck her."

"Yes. He did."

She started at his candour.

He smiled.

And then, so did she. It became an abrupt giggle, and then he found himself laughing, because sometimes, it was all that was left to do.

The tube lighting above them flickered.

"No, Norman – thank *you*."

He stared at her, confused, until he realised she was re-sponding to his earlier 'thanks'. "What for?"

The laughter faded. She smacked her lips together in an almost embarrassed fashion, and looked around her, eyes settling on the blood-filled bedpan, where his ring had found its new home, before they made their way back to him. Her smile was warm, despite the tinge of sadness that clung to it, weighing it down – weighing *her* down.

He didn't see all her armour in that second. She looked so open – simultaneously fragile and strong – just like in his hallucination of her in that field, right before he'd flung himself at her like a crazy person.

"For saving my life, with your broken marriage."

Chapter Five

She sat on the couch with Dan, watching Wayne's World on the TV. The blueish light flickered against his profile, and she looked away from him, ignoring the flutter in her stomach. He was sixteen and the next year up from her in school, but he didn't seem to mind that she was younger. What mattered most, was that he knew her mum was a drug-addict who pimped herself out in order to score, and he didn't care. He'd also never told anyone, even if everyone already knew. Once, he'd sort of shrugged and said that his brother was the same – a shitty bastard he was glad he almost never saw anymore because he'd moved out a couple of years back.

Dan's mum was never home. She worked 24/7 for some garage, so he spent his time here with her instead.

Rosa jumped a little when he laughed out loud at something in the film she'd missed.

She liked him a lot, and she wondered if he liked her too, but just wanted to play it cool. Fancying a girl in the year below him would be ammunition for all his friends for sure.

She'd overheard him tell some of them, a few weeks back, that she was like his little sister. She was like family. It had skewered her a little, but still, it was nice that he was around, even if he didn't like her that way. Better than hours alone wondering when her mum would be home next, or having to listen to what went on in her bedroom.

She leaned back, content for the moment – and moments were important. With the way that she lived, moments were all she had.

This isn't happening – it's not real. It's a memory you can't change.

She shifted uncomfortably, not sure where that voice had come from – why her mind was trying to spoil the moment.

Because you know what happens next. Do you really want to remember it?

She swallowed, suddenly feeling a little sick ... trying to scurry back into that dream space that was so comfortable, and this little corner of her past, comprised of a few hours of peace.

There's no peace...

The door slammed open and her mother's drunk, or drugged (she couldn't tell which) laughter floated into the house, along with a laugh that belonged to a man. One she didn't think she'd heard before. It sounded just as manic as her mum's.

Wake up, wake up, wake up...

Dan stiffened by her side, his eyes widening in surprise. "Shit," *he muttered.*

"What?"

"I think that's Zane."

"Who's Zane?"

"My brother – the one I told you about."

"His name's Zane?"

"Alexander. Don't ask me why or how, but it got shortened to Zane, and that name just stuck. That's what everyone calls him."

"Baby girl!" *cooed her mother walking into the room,*
one wiry, masculine arm threaded through hers and wrapped around her waist, seemingly holding her up.

Wake up, wake up, wake up...

"Daniel ... bro."

Dan smiled, nervously. It was her that Zane's eyes settled on, though. Goosebumps snaked up her back as this guy took her in. Nothing about him screamed calm and collected. He looked like a loose cannon ready to go off when you least expected it.

And his eyes pierced her where she didn't want them to.

She crossed her arms over her chest and drew her legs up on the couch a bit more.

"This your girlfriend?" he asked.

"No," said Dan. "Er ... this is Rosa. She's just a friend."

It cut her – his remark – even though she knew he meant no harm by it. Maybe she wasn't the type boys went for. She was small, and skinny, and although she kind of thought she was pretty sometimes, at fifteen, she had almost no breasts, no hips...

That didn't stop Zane from staring at the legs she'd tucked up. She wished she'd worn her leggings instead of a skirt.

"Pre-ttee Ro-sa," said Zane, accentuating every syllable.

She swallowed.

Her mother left his side and wandered into the kitchen. Next fix already?

Dan was frozen next to her.

Zane slowly moved his gaze from her to his brother. "Get lost, wimp."

She stared at Dan in shock. She'd never heard anyone speak to him like that before – certainly not his school mates, anyway. Dan was the tough guy at school. But Zane was bigger and, clearly, not to be messed with, because Dan got up and scrambled to get his shoes on.

"Dan?" she sounded, her voice hushed.

He peeked at her through his low-hanging fringe. She thought the look was apologetic, although it stayed on her no more than half a second. "Got homework to do anyway." She thought she'd heard him whisper 'sorry', but she could have been wrong.

He made his way out without saying another word.

Wake up, wake up, wake up...

She suddenly felt like a deer in headlights.

"Look at you," said Zane, his tone strangely threatening in the silence of the room, even though he hadn't raised his voice, or said anything threatening at all.

Where the hell had her mum got to? It was eight o'clock in the evening. She risked a glance towards the kitchen. She could see part-way into the open doorway and sure enough, there was her mum on the floor. It wasn't unusual for her to pass out in the kitchen at this time, especially if she'd been out all last night and today, which she had.

She could see some of her face from here. Rosa took after her in looks. Petite and blonde, with an air of fragility, her mother looked like some broken, china doll, there on the tiles, her mascara streaked down her face, her make-up now shiny and smudged.

Some strange image of an eyeless doll invaded her mind – some image that didn't belong to this memory, but another.

"Rosa, the little pixie. You look like that fairy in Peter Pan with your big eyes, and your hair all short like that. Don't usually like girls with short hair..."

Wake up!

The sofa depressed, as he knelt down on it, in front of her; practically straddling her.

She let out a gasp of fear without meaning to, annoyed she felt intimidated, because he was clearly being intimidating on purpose.

He grabbed her crossed arms and pulled them away from her chest with force. "Let me see you."

"Th-there's nothing to see."

"You're not wrong." He grabbed her left breast.

"Don't!"

The slap stung her cheek before she even knew it had been delivered. She didn't want to cry, but tears spilled down anyway.

He got right in her face, his spittle hitting her nose and chin as he shouted, "You don't EVER say 'no' to me, got it? I'm the only thing keeping Mummy-dearest happy right now. I got what she needs, but she's been pretty fucking shit at giving me what I need. Until now." *He grinned.*

She wished the couch would swallow her.

WAKE UP.

"You a virgin?"

She had to bite her tongue to keep from telling him it was none of his goddamned business. She nodded her head.

She couldn't stop it – his hand darting straight up her skirt and under her knickers – and her protest did come tumbling out this time.

He pressed his other hand against her throat, making it hard for her to breathe, as he pushed a finger inside her.

You're telling the truth. Good. Fucking miracle there's a girl your age this side of town with her flap still attached."

She whimpered.

Both hands withdrew, she inhaled, and then she was caged inside his arms which rested on the back of the sofa, either side of her head.

WAKE UP!

"Your mum's been telling me how much she misses having a strong man around the house; told me you've never known one; that she feels it's been no good for you." *He grinned again, all gnashing white teeth – at least, that's what she imagined. That's what she saw.* "I'm moving in. She loves my white powder. I'm gonna keep your mum happy ... and you're gonna keep me happy in return."

"No!"

"Hey…"

"*No.*"

"It's okay.

"No—"

"I've got you."

She lashed out – punched him where she thought his face was. Her hand did connect with something, although she wasn't sure what.

He cursed.

She blinked. So damn hard, she thought her eyelids might snap off, but she had to open her eyes and wake the fuck up. "Get your fucking hands off me!"

"Jesus, they weren't … I wasn't…"

Pitch black. It was the pitch black that confused her, until the warmth and softness beneath her brought everything back. *Christ…* "Norman?"

He groaned. "Right here."

Oh, no… "Oh, shit, I'm sorry. I'm so sorry."

They'd brought the mattress over towards the light switch, and away from the window. Norman had all but collapsed on it, shivering a little. She'd found two stained, musty blankets lying on the floor on the other side of the room, but beggars couldn't be choosers and Norman needed warmth in order to sleep and heal properly.

He'd already been out of it by the time she'd dragged the blankets over. After a moment of hesitation, she'd concluded his being warm was more important than formality, and had switched off the light and climbed on top of him, pulling the awful, scratchy blankets over them both.

Guess you fell asleep, too. "I was dreaming. I didn't realise you were you. I thought…" She trailed off. She didn't really want to talk about the dream – or memory – and telling Norman she'd thought he was Zane just seemed all kinds of wrong. He was so *not* Zane, the comparison was bordering on cruel, even if she'd thought it in her sleep.

"I've been trying to wake you. You were crying."

His worried tone pierced her. How could that be? How the hell could he be worried? He didn't even know her – how the fuck could he care?

An odd vulnerability that had nothing to do with Zane and his fists, permeated her defences. She abruptly climbed off Norman, trying to feel her way in the dark. "I didn't mean to disturb you."

"You didn't. I mean, I would probably have woken up anyway."

"You were zonked out."

"So were you."

Silence.

"Maybe..." he hesitated. "Should we turn the lights on again?"

She shrugged, until she remembered he couldn't see that. "Do you have the time on you?"

"The watch you took off..."

"Oh ... I forgot, sorry. I'll find it."

From memory, she tentatively took step after step towards where she thought the other mattresses were. The watch would be somewhere near the bedpan.

Her foot hit something that gave a little – bedding.

Getting on her hands and knees, she crawled forward, feeling her way cautiously. The last thing she wanted to do was knock that bedpan over and spill bloodied water everywhere. Luckily, her fingers scraped it before that happened. She felt around it, then beyond it ... plastic packaging, scissors, bandages... "Got it!" she smiled, her fingers closing around a metal strap.

"Fabulous. There's a night light on it if you press the dial button. It's not much – I doubt it'll light the way, but you can try."

She did, and 02:53 glowed back at her. "It's nearly three in the morning." She heard him yawn. "How are you feeling, by the way?"

"You mean, despite getting punched in the chest?"

Her face heated up, even though his tone was jovial.

"I'm teasing," he added, before she could respond. "I slept well. Thought it was for longer than just an hour and a bit."

She heard a scuffle. "What are you doing?"

"Getting up. I feel like a bloody invalid. All I've been doing is lying down, and you've done all the hard work."

"That's not true."

"Well, I feel better, anyway. The hand's sore, but it's bearable now. I'm wondering if we should try again to find a way out."

"Maybe. I dunno. If it's been this long, I think Zane scarpered. It might be easier and safer just to wait out three more hours. At least we got blankets." She didn't say she didn't want to go home. Where would she go? Back to Zane – there was nowhere else. Her mind raced a mile a minute trying to figure out how to temper him when she came face-to-face with him again. Maybe she'd go to Dan first, although she didn't know if that would make Zane angrier, or what. At least if they waited, she'd have morning on her side – she'd have light, and people, more places to go, and the potential of witnesses should he try anything else. She needed Zane to have as much time as possible to cool off, and things almost always looked better in daylight, even to someone like Zane.

She froze when the fluorescent tube flickered above them, the buzz of electricity seeming greater than before.

Norman stood by the switch. "I'll risk the lights, then."

Self-awareness cascaded over her, and she ducked her head. Maybe *some* things didn't look better in light.

She silently scolded herself for her sense of weakness. *It's 'cause of that stupid dream.* It had left her shaken, and she couldn't brush it aside.

Norman made his way towards her.

Bar the part where he'd flung them both through the window, this was the first time he'd made any kind of decisive move. For one dumbfounding moment, she had no idea what to do. Her armour went up, shrieking a red alert as it did so. Half of her wanted to run. Half of her wanted to attack. Another smaller, hidden side of her, wanted to ... respond?

This wasn't Zane, or Dan, or ... god – *any* guy she'd known. Since Zane, she hadn't known nice ones, and even Dan had had a personality transplant, going from her friend to some mostly mute yes-man for his brother as he became more and more distant from her over the years.

Norman was ... nice. Genuinely. At least, he seemed it. Not all of her believed it yet.

He stopped a couple of yards in front of her with a small smile.

It was that unfamiliar, hidden side of herself – almost a stranger – that won her internal argument. She took two steps forward and held out his watch for him.

"Thanks," he said, quietly, taking it and putting it in his pocket. Then, he walked past her, bent down, and picked up the excess strips of bandages she hadn't needed for his hand. "Come on."

Why was her heart beating so damn fast? "What?"

"Come on," he repeated, and then held out his undamaged hand for her to follow.

Awkwardly, she reached out and took it, chased by another vicious stream of arguments in her mind, that he hadn't actually intended for her to *take* his hand.

Nevertheless, he closed his around hers, and led her towards the sink.

She had a million questions. Not a single one came out.

Norman turned on the tap, it chugged, and then he held the bandages under the stream of water. He wrung the material using his one good hand, and then shut the water off.

Even though it was obvious what he had in mind, she still didn't expect it when the wet, white cloth came at her. She jumped back.

That 'deer in headlights' feeling returned, like in her dream, but this was different.

"Don't be scared," he soothed.

And she should have felt daft – him talking to her like that, like some wounded animal – but it was bloody working. Whereas Zane had made her feel nothing but fear, the only fear she felt now was *still* from Zane – his legacy – not from Norman.

"That crusted blood will start to pinch your face and hurt if we don't get it off. It can't be comfortable. Come on." But he didn't approach her – just waited.

Heart still racing its own marathon, she finally stepped back towards him.

That smile again.

Kind.

His wife had no idea what she'd had.

"It's hard with my sore hand, but I'm just going to place my arm on your shoulder – not too heavily – so I can keep us both steady. So I can clean you up properly. Okay?"

She wasn't sure if it was okay, but she nodded anyway and held her breath.

Just as promised, he kept his arm light on her right shoulder, and used it to better his stance and hers. "I hope it's not too cold."

It wasn't the cold she felt when he pressed the cloth against her cheek. It was warmth.

~*~

What the hell had she been through?

It hadn't just been a dream that had had her flailing against him – the things she had cried out...   It hadn't been much, but enough for him to form a picture of what he hoped to god hadn't happened, but knew probably had.

And when?

That, he didn't know. *It probably happened more than once.*

That was a dark thought.

The blood didn't come off her as easily as he'd like, and he was trying damn hard to make sure the fibres of the cloth didn't lift any scabs forming.

He wished he could hold her better, although he didn't know if that would be appreciated – probably not – but she was stiff as a board under his ministrations, and her wide eyes still held an element of fear.

He hated that. He'd never fucking hurt her in a thousand years, but she wasn't to know that, and he was fast suspecting 'hurt' was all she'd known from any male. Especially if they all came her way via Zane. He wondered how long he'd been in the picture for. He wondered what his role was in her life, but didn't know how to ask without coming off a complete arsehole.

"I need more water," he said, keeping his tone light and soft.

"All right," she squeaked out.

He let go of her, and leaned to the left to rinse the blood off the cloth and start again.

He noticed she followed his every movement, as if trying to guess his next one.

"Ready ... are you still okay with my arm on your shoulder?"

She stared at him in near bewilderment, but nodded again. It was funny how she'd been so in control earlier when she'd been the one giving the care. Maybe that was a more familiar part for her to play. Now, she seemed a little shell-shocked.

"It's looking much better. I've almost got all the blood off."

She was beautiful – she really was. Some of her make-up was coming off with the blood. Her eyes were so damn *blue*. And big. Her lips weren't, in fact, a vampiric red after all, but a becoming shade of pink that had him thinking of buds blooming, not the undead.

Early twenties. She couldn't be much older than that.

Far too young for you, whispered the disappointingly realistic voice in his head.

Those big eyes filled with tears.

He knocked himself out of his reverie; he shouldn't even be thinking this stuff – thinking about her in *that* way – given all the crap she'd been through tonight, let alone whatever she'd been through in her past. *Shit.* He'd scared her.

Admittedly, in spite of the circumstances, he was attracted to her – had been since the moment he'd clapped eyes on her, even if he'd been confused by the attraction. He really hoped his thoughts hadn't shown on his face just now, because he had no intentions of acting on any of them.

That's all she needs, you careless numpty.

Or maybe he was blowing this way out of proportion. Maybe he'd just been too rough with the cloth against her bruise. "Sorry ... did I hurt you?"

He'd definitely done something wrong, because her face suddenly crumpled and her tears fell – not quietly either. She cried like a dam burst – with messy force.

He had no idea what to do, so he sort of just stood still and let her make the next move, hoping she wasn't going to hit him again, unless of course, he deserved it, but he still didn't know what he'd done.

His heart ached for her.

Maybe she needed some room. He lifted his arm from her shoulder, and took a step back, only to find the front of his shirt bunched up tightly in her small hands, pulling him back.

She looked up at him, pleadingly, and he felt useless for not understanding what she was asking for.

But he couldn't do nothing, not with her staring at him like that.

Sod it.

He dropped the cloth on the floor and cupped her face with his hand in attempted comfort, hoping she'd receive it as such. He had to fight the urge to pull her towards him and hold her. As much as that felt like the most natural thing to do, he didn't want to cause her any further distress.

He didn't need to worry. She leant her cheek into his palm, and then before he saw it coming, she all but slammed her small frame against his, tucking herself into his chest, arms curling around his waist in a tight embrace, which he gladly returned.

She sobbed into his shirt, and before he could talk reason into instinct, he placed a kiss on the top of her head, and held her the best he could.

Chapter Six

She'd always loved books.

Being an urban child, and having grown into an urban adult, she'd often wondered what it would be like to live in the country, surrounded by nothing but grass and trees, under an expanse of sky never compressed by concrete structures. She hadn't even been out of the city. Ever.

London was it – the be all and end all.

Except in books, where she could run free.

She would imagine fields with grass, almost waist-high, that brushed her thighs under her dress as she walked through it. The sun would offer a warmth she'd never known outside novels and stories – the kind of books they would make her read at school when she'd been able to go. Those same books her friends had groaned at, she'd soaked up with thirst. But her schooling had been poor at best.

She had forced herself to learn to read – picked up bits and pieces, here and there, from the very few teachers who had been patient with her; from looking at words while out and about; from television, and from friends. And to avoid the shouting and drug-induced moaning, and the row of male visitors her mum would entertain, she would barricade herself in her room – there'd been no lock – and lose herself in books.

They would tell her tales of the life she could have had

if she'd been born someone else, or in a different place, perhaps to different parents, or at a different time. The possibilities were endless.

This second – and the one that came before it, and the one before that, for the last two minutes – was like a book.

At the very corner of her eye, around the edge of Norman's coat, she spied the puppet doll, cracks etched in her face, staring at the ceiling with empty sockets, reminding her this story wasn't hers. *That* one was.

Feeling more than a little stupid over the way she was acting, she thought about pulling herself away from the comfort of his body, and the care he was giving her – that had been what had set her off – yet, even knowing she should, she couldn't bring herself to let him go. Not yet. She'd have to in a few hours, but ... *not yet.* This story didn't have to end yet.

He didn't hold her loosely, but earnestly, conveying no indication he was embarrassed by her absurd show of emotion. This was a first for her. But there had been lots of firsts with this undemanding man in the space of a couple of hours.

His heartbeat against her ear filled her. That, right there, was a bit like having a piece of the sun.

"How long have you known him for?"

His question would have burst the imaginary bubble encasing them both, but he asked it tenderly, and so quietly, she wouldn't have heard were it not for the near silence surrounding them.

"Fourteen years," she replied, surprised at her willingness to. "I was fifteen. My mum brought him home, and he never moved out."

His arms around her back gripped her a little, just for a moment, and then relaxed again. "You're ... twenty-nine?"

She smiled, knowingly. "Yeah – thirty in February. I know I don't look it – I've always looked young. I kind of like it though. People are more forgiving of younger people. If they think I'm young, they cut me some slack for being with Zane – as if I don't know any better or something; or like it's somehow less my fault if I'm just a young girl."

"It's not your fault."

"That's not what people think. I can see it in their eyes, the ones who know – *why the fuck is she still with him?* That's what they're thinking. *Too weak to walk away...* As if I haven't tried."

"You tried?"

"About eight years ago. I had a friend looking to rent with a bunch of her college friends, and she was one short. She asked me if I wanted in – she even knew a guy who managed a pub and was looking for staff, so paying the rent wouldn't be a problem. She said she didn't even need a deposit from me. It was my chance – the only one I've properly had. Didn't tell Zane, or my mum, or anyone – just packed a bag one day when they were all out and left.

"I ignored their calls and texts. I wanted a new start. Only, when I turned up at the pub for my first day of work, Zane was there. He'd gone through the trash and found the number I'd scribbled down for my job interview – no name attached, but all he had to do was phone it. I should have fucking burnt it, but it didn't occur to me at the time.

"I could barely walk for a week afterwards. And just to make sure I never tried anything like that again, he beat my mum too.

"Well, I *did* try again three years ago, after my mum died – overdose, predictably. He couldn't hurt her anymore. I went straight to the police this time with bruises and cuts all over me. They took Zane in, but only held him overnight. I was stupid. The way I looked, the things I confessed ... I thought they'd keep him in for longer – a few days maybe – before bail. I thought I'd have enough time to get the fuck out. Guess their cells were full. I made it as far as Camden, where one of Dan's old school mates lived – that's where Zane found me. I hadn't planned on staying more than one night. Dan didn't know – he hadn't even kept in touch with this guy – but Dan still got in trouble.

"People don't get it. Walking away sounds easy, but it's so hard to hide your tracks, especially if someone like Zane wants to find you. Every time you try, you put everyone in danger. Staying is hell, but leaving... it's just as bad. You pick your losses, you know?"

His chin moved against her hair as he spoke. "What is he to you?"

She finally drew her arms in and stepped back from her sanctuary. She met his eyes, almost wishing she hadn't, 'cause for some reason, she really seemed to matter to him, and she just couldn't understand why. It confused the crap out of her. "What do you think he is to me?"

"Besides knowing he's bloody psychotic, I don't know what to think. What I saw in that alleyway..."

Humiliation churned. *God – take me now.* "You think ... what?" she bit out. "That he's my pimp?"

He remained silent, clearly not walking into that trap. Yeah – she was feeling it. Her inner-bitch was armed and *daring* him to call her a whore, a slut – like mother, like daughter – everything she knew everyone secretly thought.

He waited.

"I'm *not* a goddamned hooker." Her voice shook.

"I know that," he replied, without any qualm.

He held her gaze, until she blinked and looked away, crossing her arms. Her anger waned. This guy was like water – soothing, calm – yet still able to knock her off her feet in a torrent of feeling she was really not prepared for. "He's ... he thinks he's my lover, but acts like my father, although that changed a little when my mum died. After that, he became more possessive, not even able to deal with anyone looking at me. He even puts Dan through shit if he catches him looking at me in what he thinks is the 'wrong' way. What you saw, in the alleyway ... that's not usual. It's happened maybe twice before when we've had no money. His dealings have been drying up the past few months – the police are onto him, although they've yet to catch him in the act, but they've been staking out his regular patches. When he's low on cash, and if one of his regulars – who he's kinda trusting of, and all that – if they ... offer money to..." *Fuck him. Fuck Zane to kingdom come.* "That's why he did what he did."

The buzz of the lights felt like they pricked her skin.

She needed Norman to say something, but she couldn't bring herself to look at him.

"Do you love him?"

She drew her arms against herself more tightly – that wasn't a question she'd expected. "No. I don't think so. I don't know if I know what it is to love a guy, though. But I do know I hate him, and I hate him most of all, because I probably know him better than anyone else." What a twisted truth. She had never wanted Zane's intimacy.

"Does he know you?"

She raised her head and met his gaze. She had asked herself many times in the past whether she loved Zane, and in his own, distorted way, she suspected he loved her.

But she'd never once asked herself if he *knew* her.

If she'd been asked that earlier today, she wasn't sure she would have known the answer. Now, amid the cover of night, where secrets and shadows emerged – where this stranger offered her a sliver of light – it was obvious. "No. You know me better." Although she was damned if she knew how.

~*~

The door was solid oak by the looks of it. And definitely locked. There was no way he would have been able to bash it down on a good day, let alone with his busted hand. "Yep – we're locked in for the night."

He didn't miss the look of relief on Rosa's face, and he full well knew why it was there: 'cause of him. That Zane guy. She didn't want to go back to him, and from the little she'd told him earlier, it sounded like she was housed up with him, meaning there was no escape – she had nowhere else to go *except* back to him.

He'd never been an angry person by nature, but anger did simmer at the thought of *Zane*. Jesus... He never felt such disgust towards another human being.

It was on the tip of his tongue to invite her back to his bedsit. No matter how small, it was away from the psycho. But he already knew he'd have a fight on his hands convincing her, and it didn't feel quite right to mention it just yet, if at all. They were still at the 'don't know each other' phase, despite her earlier, slightly exhilarating statement that she felt he knew her.

He needed to grow the fuck up, because getting fuzzy feelings for her now would end in turmoil. This wasn't a win-win situation they were in. Rosa would go back to

Zane. Even if Norman went to the police, which he fully intended to do, with indisputable evidence about what had happened and who had done it, Zane would find her before the police found him. He wasn't a total idiot. The only way to keep her safe was to take her *completely* out of the situation, Zane being the 'situation'.

But she'd already tried that twice, and he'd found her – twice. So he'd have to find another argument to convince her to come with him once they got out of here.

And then, what, Norman? What are you going to do? What are you going to support her with? You have no money to support yourself.

He sighed. It was a fucked up world if there was no solution to this. It was fucked up that kids, women – anyone – who lived like this could be imprisoned by it. What was the fucking point of the police? Social services? There were too many rigid rules that took too long to work through, when action needed to be immediate and lasting.

"Don't sweat it," she said, misinterpreting his sigh. "We'll shout for help in the morning and it'll all be over."

He turned and leant his back against the door, letting his gaze fall on her petite frame. For him, yes, it would be over. But for her, it wouldn't be.

"We could just go back to sleep," she shrugged. "Time'll fly that way."

They both looked at the mattress with the blanket strewn on it, and an awkwardness invaded the space between them. She'd opened up to him. Entrusted him with things he wasn't sure she'd confessed to anyone else. Lying together on that bed now seemed... Well, it had lost its innocence, put it that way. Especially because this time, he wouldn't be asleep. Feeling her pressed up against him whilst *awake*... He wasn't sure he'd be able to hide his attraction, and she really didn't need that from him.

"Why did your wife cheat on you?"

His breath caught in his throat. Shit. Turned out, it still hurt – the memory of walking in on her – although, the hurt over *her* was a bit less. Less in his heart. Where he felt the pain was in his gut and he suspected it was more to do with his bruised ego – the humiliation of being cuckolded.

He let his breath out, cautiously. Yes... his chest felt a little freer than of late. "I'm not sure I know the whole answer. She said we'd been having problems for a long time – that I didn't listen to her. There were parts about her past she missed, that I couldn't help her find again, and this guy I walked in on her with ... I dunno. Maybe he could. He's that dynamic sort, you know?"

She looked at him quizzically. "Dynamic?"

"Yeah ... you know..."

She let out a small laugh, then shook her head.

"Dynamic. Exuberant personality, good to look at, confident..."

She wrinkled her nose at him. God, that was cute. "You're saying that like you're ... not dynamic?"

He didn't mean to let out the chortle-laugh-snort thing he just did. "I'm not. I'm ... 'normal Norman'."

Now, she looked like she was about to tease him without mercy. "Normal Norman?" she asked, incredulously.

He felt his neck heat up. He shouldn't have bloody said anything because any respect she might have had for him was one second short of disintegrating. "Look, I was the fat nerd at school – smart enough, but quiet. I was the one who did all his work on time and kept his head down so he wouldn't get unwanted attention. I was the one no one would sit next to by choice, just 'cause *someone* has to be that guy and it was me. The boys all wanted me to do their homework. The girls would all joke about how I fancied them, even though I didn't, and make very dramatic, loud plans to constantly avoid me. I learnt that if I just kept quiet and invisible, people paid less attention to me and my day went by better, so I did – keep quiet and invisible, I mean. Quiet and invisible. Not dynamic."

She just stared at him with that same bemused look on her face.

Even though he was a full grown adult now, old habits died hard, and he found himself waiting for the subtle jibes to start.

"Don't do that," she said.

"Don't do what?"

"Judge me."

He raised his brows, surprised, but although her words were harsh, her tone was light, and she still wore a small smile. "I can see it in your face. I'm not one of those girls – wasn't, I mean. That's not who I was at school."

He had to take a mental step back, and out of himself. Out of the years-old lessons that shaped who you were without you realising it. She wouldn't have had those tattoos and dreadlocks at school, and that, he realised, was what he was basing his impromptu revisit to his teens on: how she looked. A surface thing. But he already knew she wasn't like that. He'd seen beyond all that earlier tonight, and he hated that she didn't know that.

"I didn't mean to judge you," he said, sincerely.

"I know."

"It's just, the past is sometimes so—"

"I know."

Her smile widened in understanding.

A mutual acceptance danced on the pause that stretched before them.

She was the first to break it. "So ... all that quiet studying you did... You a rocket scientist now?"

He laughed.

She grinned.

"No. I, er ... I wanted to be a veterinarian – always loved animals – but I didn't quite make the grades for the medical studies. Ended up working in data and analysis for a marketing company – office job. I lost that the same day I lost my wife – was made redundant. I met Tina young, and she fell pregnant shortly after I left college, so, needs other than fanciful dreams came first."

"You ... have kids?"

"Two girls. Twelve and Fifteen. Never thought I'd miss their loud chatter as much as I do. That's the hardest part about the break-up – losing them. Well ... I haven't lost them, per se, but I've certainly lost time with them, and they're hurting, too. It'll take a while for things to be okay between them and me, if they ever are again."

"But your wife's the one who ended it."

"That's neither here nor there where the kids' care and well-being are concerned. She's still their mother."

"Oh."

"Divorce is a messy thing."

"I'm sorry."

"Don't be. Some people have it worse."

Her smile faded. She tore her eyes from his, cast them around the room and took a sharp breath. "Maybe there's an exit we missed."

Something rustled.

They both froze, and Norman's hairs rose on the back of his neck.

Rosa didn't move a muscle, but stared at him with wide-eyed fright.

It darted across her feet – something small and brown – and Rosa screamed, leaping a foot into the air.

He couldn't one hundred percent say he hadn't screamed either – there had certainly been a scream in his head. Scurrying, furry things topped off the 'freakish infirmary' feel nicely.

She was in his arms before he could blink, her back to him so she could see where whatever-the-hell-it-was had got to.

"Mouse," he said, trying to calm himself down.

"Rat!"

"Too small."

"It didn't look fucking small!"

"It was, I promise. Just a mouse."

"This is London – we get rats."

"Hey..." He wrapped his good arm around her waist to stop her jittering, not least because he was suddenly, and unexpectedly, too aware of her backside rubbing into his crotch. The heat inside him tripled; the only good thing about that being it kept him a little warmer against the December cold and lack of heating.

"Where did it go?" she asked, her voice high.

"I don't know."

"Not near the bed, right?"

"I don't think so."

"Any chance you can sound more certain?"

"We can always pull out another mattress." And to hell with it – the thought of beds and lying down with her, coupled with the *feel* of her, right where he shouldn't be feeling her...

He tried to push her forwards, away from him, but she

was having none of it, still looking wildly across the floor for the little pest. Her hands gripped his arm as she pressed herself further *into* him.

Jesus Christ. He needed to get her off, before it was—

Her movements ceased.

He inwardly groaned, feeling every bit the jerk, 'cause there was *no way* she wasn't able to feel his semi-erection against her.

Rosa turned in his arms, slowly.

He had nowhere to hide.

Her face expressed her shock.

There was nothing for it but honesty. *Fuck.* "Er ... look, I'm sorry." Well, this was fun. "It's just..." His heart was in his damn throat, embarrassment just about to swallow him whole. "You were up against me, and—"

"Do you *like* me?"

Was she fucking kidding? His entire head was on fire from the neck up – probably. She hadn't moved away from him, not even a little, and his damn dick was still in happy mode because the idea of them together had somehow planted itself into his DNA. Clearly, rats, blood, and being shot at weren't enough kill the mood. Ha. "Erm..." He gave up, nodded, then hung his head in defeat and an attempt at an apology. "I liked you when I first saw you, back at the pub. You were running around like a ferret, and everything about you was—" *Norman, don't tell a woman she reminds you of a ferret—* "Er ... not ferret. I meant, um—"

You're shit at this.

He let out a long sigh. "You don't have to worry, okay? I'm not going to act on it."

She was as still as a statue.

"If, um, you could maybe move away from me..." 'Cause that was a near full-sized boner in his pants now, and he could do fuck all about it if she insisted on leaning against it. What in god's name was wrong with his body? Perhaps this was some kind of physiological compensation that had grounding in science, or something: draw blood to penis so broken hand can feel better.

Yes, Norman, very scientific.

"What if I don't want to move away?"

It took him quite a few seconds to register what she'd said – barely audible; barely a whisper... His mind jumped straight on the hallelujah-bandwagon, but thankfully, there was still some blood left in the upper part of his body, feeding oxygen to brain cells. "We really shouldn't—"

"God," she butted her head into his chest, "I'm so angry with myself."

"What? Why?"

"Because ... this is my mess I dragged you into, and you don't deserve any of it, and I feel like I'm ruining you with every single thing I say, and..." she lifted her head, eyes shimmering, "I'm a selfish, selfish bitch. Because all I can think about, is whether I'll regret it in three hours, when we walk out of here, and I never know, not even once, what it's like to be with a really nice guy."

She ducked her head again, and wiped her cheek on the back of her hand; then, she finally stepped back. "I'm sorry. Shit."

She turned her back on him, heading towards the other side of the room.

Her withdrawal hit him like a freight train. The fact that she might actually be equally attracted to him, was oncoming freight train number two.

But they really, *really* shouldn't... "You've *never* been with someone who treats you right?"

He saw the back of her head shake. "Fifteen – remember? That's how old I was when Zane... It's always been Zane. Just Zane. I'm sorry again."

"You don't need to—"

There was a rattle along the ground above them, outside – a can being kicked.

"Shit!" gasped Rosa. She leapt for the light switch.

They were plunged into darkness before he could move, and he regretted in that second letting her walk away from him, because he wanted to be holding her right now; protecting her. "Rosa..." he whispered.

"Ssshhhhh."

He held his breath and she must've been doing the same, because he couldn't hear her at all. Nothing. He didn't like it.

Praying he wouldn't knock anything over, he began to make his way to where he thought she was, one painstakingly slow step at a time.

Whatever noise they'd heard above them had stopped now, but *someone* had still created it. Someone was up there, and since they could hear no voices, it was probably someone on their own.

Another step in the dark... Where was she? Had she moved again?

Something soft bumped into his arm, and on instinct alone he grabbed it.

She made a muffled noise.

"It's me." He pulled her straight into his chest, relief pouring off him.

"Norman," she whispered, her lips against his neck.

He hugged her tighter, and they both stood there in silence, waiting. He had no idea how many minutes had passed, but it had to have been nearer ten before they finally relaxed, no further sounds filtering down from the outside world.

"Just someone walking by," he whispered.

Her frame began to shake.

"We're fine," he soothed. "He's not coming. I'm not going to let him do anything to you."

"Norman..." she whispered again.

Arms wrapped around his neck as she rose against him. A wet cheek met his nose as she placed a kiss on the side of his face.

A second one landed a bit lower down against his jaw, and it wasn't hard – not hard at all – to follow the trail of her sweet breath towards her lips, until her mouth met his.

Chapter Seven

It wasn't the first time she'd been kissed, but it might as well have been, because *this*, she wanted – too much to be sensible. And the 'want' was in full force, cascading through her mind and body, and overshadowing all else; initiating an unfamiliar, tightening ache she needed to soothe – needed *him* to soothe.

Like everything else about him, his lips – his kiss – was soft, but quickly deepened as he took her into him with a quiet sigh. And he *was* taking her into him – this was just like falling, only the landing promised to be worth it.

Tenderness laced every movement he made; every stroke of his tongue against hers. It was a wonderful novelty. She'd never known tenderness – not in this way – and she returned it with a fuelling passion she didn't know she was capable of feeling for a man, winding her arms tighter around his neck as her hands sought out further softness in the tufts of his hair.

He pulled back, and she lost the touch of his mouth on hers. It was like he took the air with him. "Don't stop," she gasped out. "Please don't."

"Your bruise... I don't want to hurt you."

"Losing you's the only thing that hurts." That wasn't quite what she'd meant to say. She'd meant to say losing the *feel of him* was what hurt, but that was too many words to formulate when battling with the immediacy with which she needed him back.

However he interpreted it, the result was to her liking. His tongue met hers again, her lips already open for his, drinking him in...

Only when her feet hit their mattress did she realise they'd been moving in the dark.

His fingers worked their way under her coat and thin jumper until their tips met the skin at her waistline, causing a shiver to snake up her spine. Her damn coat could come off.

"You'll freeze," he protested as she impatiently tugged at it.

"I won't." All she could feel was heat. She pulled him back against her and his hand went under her top once more, with more ease this time, higher up against her back, and she just wanted him to stay there – never wanted to lose his touch again. *And what about his injured hand?* Oh ... selfish... "Your hand."

"Hmmm?" He murmured the half-question against her mouth, still kissing her.

"The one that hurts."

"All I feel is you." He went down on his knees, lifting her jumper up, and branded her abdomen with kisses. His tongue flicked lightly across the metal bar decorating her navel, the short hairs of his beard tickling her as he moved.

She threaded her fingers through his hair; surprisingly thick and a little long, and she sensed him looking up at her, even though she couldn't see a damn thing. "I want the lights back on," she said suddenly, needing the magic of this moment to be everything it could be. She needed to *see*.

His hand dropped from her waist, and she stepped to

the left around the mattress, feeling for the wall and the light switch. When she found it, she pressed it down, and then turned to face him as the blueish hue filtered into the room, flicker by flicker.

Still on his knees, he looked like some kind of gift she didn't deserve, and almost Christ-like with his halo of brown hair and beard; a look of adoration on his face she'd never once been the cause of for anyone.

He smiled, reached his hand out to her; then a too-loud buzz filled the room – she could practically *feel* the chaotic electricity on her skin – and with a small 'ping' that resonated against glass, the lights went out completely.

Her fear went up, along with some eerie foreboding she couldn't shake off. "Norman?"

"Here..." She heard him make his way to her, and then she was in his arms again, sinking into him and hoping to god she didn't drown. "Guess the light broke. Sounds like the bulb went."

She still felt uneasy. "I wanted us to be able to see."

"I can see."

"You can?"

His thumb grazed her left wrist. "You have red roses here, on both wrists, bleeding petals, hiding bruises underneath." He slid his finger up her arm, stopping half way to her elbow. "There's a skull here, sockets peeking through green leaves that rise to hold up an open lotus – a frog on one side of it, a snake on the other. Your other arm, in the same place, shows a cross nailed to Christ, rather than Christ nailed to the cross; holly and ivy entwining around both. Above that, you have a—"

She clamped a hand on his mouth.

Unable to speak words, tears fell instead, and she

shook her head, both in wonderment, and in sorrow so deep it defied explanation.

Releasing her grip just a little, she stroked his lips with her thumb.

"I see you, Rosa," he whispered.

"Make love to me." Her heart thudded in her ears like hoof beats bearing the apocalypse. *What the hell...? What the* hell *did I just say?!*

But she couldn't *not* have said it – not when this was it. Right now. The only chance they'd ever get.

Don't fool yourself. This is just a moment, that's all. Like all the others. And like all the others, it'll be over in a heartbeat. It's a fleeting second – you won't be able to hold onto this...

She closed her eyes against her darkest voice; against every minute of every hour she'd ever been afraid to hope for anything. *You won't be able to go back – you know that, right? If you do this, nothing will ever be the same again.*

Some moments were worth changing everything for.

She felt his breath against her cheek; his heat against her hip. His voice hitched. "Are you ... sure?"

"No one ever has. I don't know what that's like. I want to know. I want to know it with you."

Far too much time passed in the silence of the next few seconds that followed, and she almost took it all back; almost caved to the darkness that let fear keep her safe.

Not a day in your life have you been safe.

His mouth crashed down on hers, all tenderness now underlined with a powerful certainty that took over his every action, and stole her breath away.

~*~

Norman wasn't sure if he was on his way to heaven, or on

his way to hell.

Exactly ten seconds ago, it didn't matter anymore, because like the strange circumstances that got him into this mess in the first place, it was Rosa's happiness that mattered, no matter how fleeting; the unerring certainty she deserved it – deserved *more* than life had dished out for her.

He wondered if he was under some delusion he could save her. Perhaps who he was really saving, was himself – from two months of debilitating hopelessness and a future he hadn't planned for.

The fact that he fancied the pants off her helped. Or didn't help, depending on which way you looked at it.

But when all else was stripped away, what remained was that he *wanted* her, and she – miraculously – wanted him back. And they had three hours before whatever forces threw them together, pulled them apart again. Urgency added a heady level of intensity to the moment.

He wished he could strip her, but she really would freeze.

His hand, delighting in the smooth flesh of her stomach, trailed upwards and grazed the tip of her breast through a lacy bra. Her nipple was rock hard under the pad of his thumb, causing the ache below his navel to deepen, and her back to arch under his touch as she let out a small whimper.

God, help me... "Just say 'stop' and I will," he muttered into her neck, dipping his tongue into its hollow.

She nodded and pressed herself into him; was practically climbing up him.

"Come here..." He guided her back to where he hoped the mattress was until his toe nudged its side. Cursing the futility of his left hand, he levered himself down with his right one 'til he was sitting. Reaching forward, he pulled her on top of him.

Heaven, he decided. He was going to heaven, because the perfect fit of her body slotted against his was such.

Groin to groin, he heard her groan – his own groan not far behind – at the feel of him between her thighs.

He pulled that jumper of hers right up to her shoulders, cupped his prize, squeezed it plump, then sealed his mouth around cotton lace, and her entire left breast.

"Jeeesus," she moaned, while he tongued and sucked and flicked at every sensitive spot he could find. When he'd soaked the lace through, he pulled the cup of her bra down over her breast and started all over again.

She bucked against his straining cock.

Her right breast received the same treatment as she fisted her hands in his hair and pulled. Those hands finally let him go and moved down his face, his neck, his chest...

He gave her nipple a last tug with his teeth, before leaving a kiss on it, and moved back up her throat as her hands settled on his waist.

There was a sharp pull at his trouser button, and it came undone.

His cock jerked. He wondered if she felt it against her crotch. She slid back a bit to make more room for her hands. The zip came down next, although he had to sit up a bit to ensure it came down smoothly.

Before he could think about the next move, the front of his underwear was pulled down as far as it would go, releasing his erection to the chilly air. It slapped his belly softly, seeping with need. "Rosa..." he moaned, not really knowing what he was going to say next.

Her hand came down on it, and his moan got a hell of a

lot louder.

"You're slippery," she stated, her quiet voice, husky.

"You turn me on so fucking much," he replied.

After a pause he couldn't decipher, she leaned forward, found his lips, and kissed him softly.

Heaven became a little too close when she tightened her fingers around his shaft and stroked downwards – hard – a complete contrast to the tender stroking of her tongue inside his mouth.

He grabbed her wrist before she could continue. "Honey ... too good. It's too good. If you want me to make love to you, you need to stop."

She sounded her disappointment.

"Wait..." He reached into the inside pocket of his coat with his right hand, and pulled out his wallet. Clumsily, with his one hand, he opened it, resting it between Rosa and himself, and fumbled with one of the little compartments inside.

"What are you doing?"

"I've got a condom in my wallet. And I really fucking hope it's not out of date."

She laughed.

He grinned. "Got it." He slipped it between his teeth and chucked the wallet aside, then he handed it to Rosa. "You'll have to help me put it on."

"Gladly." The light, sexy teasing of her tone stoked his fire.

"I want this off first," he growled, tugging at her jeans.

"Also not a problem." She stood and stripped, and yeah – bloody lights. Not being able to view this treat was a goddamned travesty. But he wasn't going to be outdone by old electrical circuits. Even standing, she still straddled him, and once he heard those boots and jeans come off, he reached up, gliding his hand up her thigh. "Let me."

She took his hand and guided it up towards the top of her knickers. They felt lacy too, and fuck – he could smell her. Musky, and sweet and aroused.

He let out a soft groan and stopped at her pubic mound, passing the pad of his thumb over it.

She gasped, and he just couldn't help himself – all that damn heat coming off her – he slipped his thumb under the seat of her panties and slid against beautiful wetness.

Her gasp turned into an audible cry.

Too fucking good.

And two fingers went in. His very patient penis throbbed at the promise of exactly what it would feel like to be inside her. He wasn't going to last. He was *way* out of practice, and fuck his other hand for being out of commission. He wanted to touch her everywhere – it was just going to have to take twice as long.

She moaned and rocked her hips when he began to thrust. It was almost hypnotic – the feel of her, the sound of her, every movement from her; every tantalisingly torturous quiver around his fingers. He wondered what she tasted like; wondered if now was a good time to find out, or if changing step would ruin this perfect pace they'd somehow set.

She pulled him right out of his dazed thoughts with something he hadn't fully expected. She uttered a sound of complete surprise, grabbed his hair almost painfully, dug her nails into his arm, and for one horrendous moment he thought he'd hurt her, until he realised she was on the brink of orgasm.

Shit.

He slid in as deep as he could and picked up his pace just a fraction.

Her breath hitched on a ferocious gasp. "God ... what... uuuh..."

He moaned along with her, gritting his teeth and hoping to all the powers that be he wouldn't just shoot off with her, 'cause by god, he could. "Come, baby ... come."

The magic words.

She bore down on his fingers, clenched, wailed, clenched, rocked, clenched ... trembled all around him as her release filled the darkness.

He froze when he heard tears. She was crying? Good crying, or bad crying?

Holy mother of... "Rosa ... sweetheart..."

She moved ferociously, almost leaping from him, and he never wished he could see her face more than at this second. "What did I do? What happened?"

There was the soft sound of material shifting against skin.

Foil ripped.

The condom? "Rosa..."

Quiet sobs pierced the blackness and his heart. "Fuck ... please talk to me."

Her weight landed on him, and her lips smashed onto his, urgently, savagely.

He hissed into her mouth when she made contact with his cock, rubber over the tip as she pinched and rolled the condom down. But she still wasn't saying a bloody thing.

"Rosa," he demanded, frustration seeping into his fear.

She pulled back from his lips and leant her cheek against his; then, she whispered in his ear, timidly; fragmented... "I've never come before."

She ... *whaaaaat?*

"Not once. Never."

He was stunned. He had no idea what to say, and then

it didn't matter because her velvety warmth was enveloping him as she lowered herself onto him.

Some abstract noise left him, the sensation of her body surrounding his, all-consuming.

Never come... That was the first time she'd ever...

No fucking way was it going to be the last.

He groaned as she started to move herself up and down his length – divine was an understatement – but he reached for the back of her neck and brought her head down, slowing *everything* down as he leant up for another kiss.

"It's your turn," she protested.

"You don't have to worry about that; I've been close ever since we started. I'm definitely going to come."

"Then why—" She yelped as he dropped himself backwards on the mattress, taking her with him. Then, he pushed his hips up, into her, deeply.

She moaned.

"Like this."

"Okay," she breathed out.

He pulled her jumper up, wanting those irresistible, perfectly-sized breasts in his mouth again, and that's where they went.

Sinking into her in every way he could, he set the pace once more, from beneath.

His good arm held her close, wrapped around her waist, encouraging her to move, which she did with abandon.

His lips moved up her neck until they found her mouth again.

She took the extra leverage from his altered position and rode him – wildly, powerfully... nothing about her efforts was hesitant or feeble.

"You're beautiful," he uttered.

Her forehead met his, and he thought he caught the glimmer of her eye. "So are you."

The first wave of bliss uncoiled from his navel, putting pressure on all the right places. He reached between them and squeezed the base of his dick as hard as he could, dispersing that sweet ache for another minute... *Uuhhh - maybe not that long.*

He moved his hand up and found her clit.

She babbled two syllables he couldn't decipher, then, "Norman..."

He said nothing, because he couldn't say anything. Any amount of energy driven into anything other than what he was focused on, would have him letting go too soon.

He kept his touch light, but steady, taking his cues from every sound she made; every ripple she gave...

Sod it – he was too close ... he was too—

"Norman!"

She climaxed. Again.

Above him, around him, on him, all over him... *Thank god!* He finally erupted. Fucking detonated inside her, the force of his release triggering a near astral projection experience...

...floating...

He didn't have to slip out of her to know he'd filled the damn condom.

She collapsed on top of him, their sated breaths the only sound in the room.

When they eventually eased, he kissed the top of her head, stroking her side. "Are you all right?"

It took longer than he'd like for her to respond. When she finally did, her words made him soar. But the anguish in her voice was a bullet of its own.

"You're the best thing that's ever happened to me." She tightened her arms around him, still sheathing him, and pressed herself into him. "When this ends, I don't know how I'm going to go back."

Chapter Eight

She ran. Laughed. The world was hers and because it was hers, no one could hurt her – no one was allowed to.

She usually ran alone in her dreams. This time, however, she wasn't alone. Far off to her left someone else ran with her.

Norman?

But he seemed less at ease than she. In fact, he looked like he was panicking; trying to call her attention to something.

She was so fully concentrated on him, and wondering why he wasn't running beside her, that she almost didn't see the figure right in front of her.

She came to a shrieking halt, stopping just short of flying into...

Terror gripped her. A stone-cold sinking pulled at her stomach, taking her down, as if to her grave.

The life-sized porcelain doll stood in front of her, face cracked and eyeless. Yet, it stared at her through empty sockets as if it knew her. Strings hung off it in a disarrayed fashion; not just a doll – a puppet.

Norman shouted her name in the distance, and ... what was he saying?

But she couldn't take her eyes off the doll.

It smiled. Its face cracked more. "My name is Rosa," it said. "What's yours?"

Vomit surged up her throat from the pit of her sinking stomach. "No. You're not Rosa."

"*I am.*"

"*No. No, you're not.*"

"*Rosa!*" yelled Norman.

But which Rosa was he calling?

It didn't matter. He was safety and warmth and all things good. This doll was everything that was wrong.

She stepped back and turned to run to him, when she was yanked back by her wrists. Looking down, the horror grew when she saw she was bound by the strings of the puppet, wound around her wrists ... cutting into her...

"*You can't run this time.*"

This wasn't happening. "*No ... I—*"

"*Look.*" *The doll pointed, and she followed the outstretched hand.*

There was a couch in the middle of the field. Zane had her pinned to it as he raped her.

She shut her eyes against the memory.

"*We never forget our firsts,*" *taunted the doll.*

The first, the second, fifth, tenth, the every...

"*I don't want to see this,*" *she pleaded.* "*Why? Why are you showing me?*"

Nervously, she glanced at Norman. She didn't want him to see this either, but he wasn't looking that way - he was looking at her. Waiting.

Waiting for what?

A door slammed, even though there was no door in the middle of the field. She looked around frantically. Who? Who was there? She saw no one.

"*You have to do it!*" *Norman called out.*

She looked at him, desperately. Do what?

"*You can't run from everything that makes you who you are,*" *said the doll, gleefully.*

Rage uncoiled like a dragon. "That's not what makes me,"

she hissed.

It giggled – this eerie, girlish sound that dug under her skin and crawled like worms. "Liar, liar, pants on fire..."

"Free yourself!" shouted Norman.

I do ... I do want to...

"No, you don't," tinkered the doll, its porcelain voice light and sharp. The bindings on her tightened, making her whimper. "You want to die."

"I don't want to die," she whispered in reply.

"Death is the only thing you've ever wanted – to die and to fly into a story better than yours. The only true freedom, is death."

No, protested her mind, but without conviction, for she couldn't escape the truth: she had wished for death so many times in the past.

"And just two hours ago when you awoke—"

Zane—

"—from unwanted hands binding yours."

She cried out when the string cut skin. Blood seeped.

"Your mother always told you, remember? In moments of drunkenness, at the end of her tether, unable to cope – how you were born with the cord around your neck. How you should have died. How she wished you had."

"Rosa..."

Norman? She turned to face him, and saw him standing a bit closer, but still some metres away. He's waiting for me.

"He's waiting for you to die."

A sob broke free as the strings cut even deeper and blood met grass. "No..." He's waiting for me to live. But she couldn't say that out loud. What if it wasn't true? What if this was just another book?

"Rosa..."

Everything swam as her life force dripped from her pulsing

wrists.

"That's it ... so peaceful, isn't it? Just close your eyes ... forget it all..."

"Rosa..."

He was waiting...

"...forget it all..."

"No..."

"Yes..."

She fell to her knees, her legs too weak to hold her up any longer.

There it was again – a door slamming. But this time, as she fell forward and her cheek met the ground, she saw the door. It stood there, hinged to nothing, in the middle of the field. Despite it being slammed, it stood ajar. Golden light beamed from the open gap.

"I don't want to die," she forced out with every ounce of strength left in her.

Fingers curled around its edge from the other side, sending her dying pulse leaping, and the door began to open...

~*~

"Rosa..."

Her eyes snapped open on a gasp.

"Don't hit me this time, okay?"

"Norman...?"

"Right here."

Relief washed over her like a tidal wave. She reached for his lips with hers, and sighed into his mouth when they met.

He smiled against her kiss and let out a sigh of his own. "That's better than a punch."

"I'll never hit you again. I loathe that I did that."

"Hush ... I know you were asleep – you didn't mean it."

"That's no excuse."

"It's a valid reason, not an excuse."

She curled up into him, under the blankets. "You're so warm. I never want to get up again."

"It's four-thirty. We have ninety minutes left."

Sorrow dug deeper than she ever thought it could, and it was a perplexing sadness that it created, filled with un-answered what-ifs and unfulfilled happiness. "Is that all? Did you check?"

"Just now. While I was trying to wake you up. You were having another bad dream."

She levered herself up above him, barely able to make out his features in the darkness. "Did you hear something? Like a door slamming?"

"You mean down here? No."

"Did you hear anything at all?"

"Just you mumbling things I couldn't understand. Are you all right?"

She couldn't shake the uneasiness she felt. "A little spooked from the dream, that's all."

"Well, this is a bit of a spooky place."

Wasn't that the truth.

"Wait 'til the dawn comes in. Everything looks better in the light."

"Part of me doesn't want morning to come," she con-fessed, falling back into the safety of his arms.

"I know what you mean." He took a breath, his chest moving hers as it rose. "I was thinking ... come stay with me."

Her own breath got stuck, the possibility of doing such a thing both beautiful and deadly.

"It's just a small bedsit, and I'm only in it until March,

but it's ... I don't know what it is, to be honest, but it's an opportunity – a chance."

"Where are you going in March?"

He paused. "Abroad."

"Really? Where? Why?"

"Don't laugh, okay?"

Intrigued, she looked up, trying to make out his face again.

"Remember I said I wanted to be a veterinarian? Well, I haven't got the training for that, obviously, but I found an animal charity looking for workers to go to Kenya to help with conservation in safari parks and sanctuaries. Very little pay, but they provide the training and accommodation. It's six months to start with and then I can decide whether to stay on or come back. But all my money runs out in April, so ... this is sort of a leap of faith. Figured it would look good on my very boring CV, and maybe this non-dynamic forty-year-old can go on to work with animals here afterwards, somehow or another – with some experience behind him."

"Wow. That's ... so cool. And I don't know why you keep saying that."

"Saying what?"

"About you not being dynamic." She pressed a kiss into his neck. "You took a bullet for me and saved my life. You're the most dynamic person I know. I don't know anyone else who would have done what you did. Most guys who heard what you heard in that alleyway, would have gotten the hell out of there. I still don't know why you didn't."

His hand felt so good, right there, stroking her lower back. How had she lived thirty years and never known this before? She'd missed out big time. *Other people are allowed this, not you.*

She blinked back a surge of tears and blocked out the debilitating voice that had forever held her captive.

I've held you safe.

No, she argued, silently. *You held me caged.*

"I had a vision of you," he said, quietly.

"What do you mean?"

"Exactly that. In the alleyway ... I didn't see you the way you think I saw you. I saw ... this is gonna sound weird, but ... you were standing in a field, the sun shining on you and all your tattoos, bringing everything about you to life, and you looked so beautiful and free... That's why I did it. I had this image of you I can't explain, and I wanted that image to be real – for you to have that. And maybe there was other stuff," he snorted a little, "like suppressed anger at my wife, and so on. Who knows why we do what we do when faced with life and death, and only a second to process it." His hand stilled on her back. "Is that weird? About the vision? I didn't want to creep you out."

She smiled, and dropped a kiss against his ear. "Dynamic Norman," she whispered.

He laughed, and turned his head to catch her mouth.

This kiss was deep, intoxicating, and tugged at the sorrow in her heart for everything she couldn't have.

"So ... will you come stay with me?"

"No."

"Fuck ... Rosa—"

"He'll find me, because he always does, which means he'll find you. I won't put you in danger."

"It's only 'til March, and then—"

"Norman, no—"

"And then, come to Kenya with me."

Her eyes widened in shock. "Come to ... what?"

"You said you've never been anywhere. So, why not?"

"I ... I don't even have a passport. I—"

"So get one. Apply now, it'll be ready before March."

"I don't—"

"Do you like animals?"

She stalled. Couldn't believe he was saying these things – *giving* her these things – despite everything. "I love animals, but—"

"Don't say no because of Zane."

She fell silent.

"I don't care how dangerous he is; how fucking deranged ... he's not worth it. He's not *worth* being the reason you say no to this. Say no because you hate the idea, because it would be the sensible thing to do since you don't know me at all; because you don't want to travel; because of anything else you might be leaving behind – but not because of him."

She couldn't form words, but he seemed to be answering every question in her mind anyway, sometimes even before it manifested.

"I don't know what we're doing here – you and me ... I don't know what we are or what we can be, but this doesn't have to be about that. This can just be about ... a chance. Taking a chance."

A chance. That's what this was – *a chance.*

Hope filled her, along with every wonderful thing about this man.

"I can't make the decision for you – you have to do it."

SAY YES, shouted some distant version of herself, peeking out through bars... The word – perhaps the whole world – was right there, on the tip of her tongue; one life-changing word, riding on one leap of faith...

Somewhere outside the room, down some hall beyond

their reach, a door slammed.

~*~

She froze above him, in his arms; him still silently pleading her to say yes; to take one more chance and hope that 'third time lucky' was a very real thing for her.

"Did you hear that?" she whispered, fear pouring off her.

"Yes." *Shit.* He broke out in goosebumps, but his fear didn't quite match hers yet – he was so close. *She* was so close to breaking free. All she had to do was say—

"Rooooosssaaaaa..."

Now the fear kicked in.

Zane.

Rosa let out a small noise of terror that seemed more animal than human.

She scrambled off him, reaching for clothes as he did the same, both of them pitching speed against being as quiet as possible.

"You down here, Rosa?"

As soon as he found out this door was locked, this is where he'd assume they were. Norman doubted he'd leave without trying to break the door down. If he still had a gun, one shot at the lock would do it.

Muted trembling sobs came from Rosa as she struggled with what he thought was her boot. He buttoned his trousers, then grabbed her arm. "I meant what I said – I'm not going to let him hurt you."

He wouldn't. How could he live with himself if he did?

"Say yes, Rosa," he whispered. "Say, you'll come with me."

He sensed, rather than saw, her looking at him,

stunned. At least it ceased her crying.

He felt her shake her head. He couldn't tell if that was a 'no', or just a reaction of disbelief, but it frustrated him. He needed her to have something to hang onto. He needed her to believe they'd get out of here. *He* needed to believe they'd get out of here.

"Rosa!"

God damn it...

"I saw the lights on earlier, you stupid bitch."

Norman's anger tightened inside him. Hadn't they seen a storage cupboard in here earlier?

He pulled Rosa along behind him, feeling for the way.

"Norman..." she breathed out, sharply.

"Storage cupboard."

They made it there with minimal sound, not that that would make much difference. It was only a matter of time before Zane found this room, and judging by the distance of his voice, that time was almost up.

Norman felt for the lock, pulled it back by its lever, and then opened the cupboard.

The handle to the door of the room turned.

They both stood stock still and held their breath.

After a moment, Zane slammed the door with his fist. "ROSA!"

She jumped, let out this little mewl of terror, and Norman pushed them both into the cupboard.

He hugged her tight. She wasn't going to like this one bit, but he couldn't see another way.

Blocking every single thing wrong with the world right out, he thought of nothing but the need to know what she felt like again; what she tasted like; and yes – the need to fix every broken thing about her... He took her in a kiss, lasting all of three seconds. It would have to be enough.

"Don't move a muscle; don't say a fucking word," he told her, before he stepped out the cupboard, and locked her in.

~*~

"Don't move a muscle; don't say a fucking word."

Too late. She caught on to his intention far too late.

"No..." She lunged forward, grabbing air instead of his sleeve, as she heard the door shut and the lock slide into place. "Norman!" she hissed as loudly as she dared. What the hell did he think he was doing?

But she already knew the answer. He was putting himself in the line of fire – again. If Zane saw him, he wouldn't look for her, especially if he made out she wasn't here.

"Norman," she cried, louder this time, "No."

"ROSA..." Zane still banging at the door.

Then, it went quiet.

The kind of quiet that cut through everything.

She clamped both hands on her mouth to stop sobs from tumbling out. Tears brimmed over her lids and streamed down her cheeks.

She wanted to be with Norman. She didn't want him out there on his own, but she suddenly didn't know what to do. Would he be safer if she surrendered herself to Zane? Or would Zane kill him the moment he had her again?

A deafening, explosive BANG tore through the darkness.

Her hands moved to clamp her ears instead of her mouth, and she had to bite her tongue to keep from screaming. She tasted blood.

He's shot the lock, he's shot the lock...

NORMAN! shrieked her mind. Never in her life had she wanted to keep anyone safe so badly, not even Dan; not even her mum. Whatever they meant to her, they'd had a hand in creating their own mess. Norman had walked into hers, and that just wasn't fair. It wasn't okay – not in any universe, book, or story.

Where was he? What was he doing?

"She's not here," came his voice, low and steady – way steadier than she'd ever felt in her life. Just hearing him flamed her relief. And her desperate worry.

It sounded like Norman was across the room again, maybe as far as the window, by the mattresses they'd landed on.

She heard Zane growl, and then stride across the room, cocking the hammer back on the gun.

She forced herself not to make a sound as her mind ran a mile a minute. He had a revolver – six bullets in the cylinder. He'd gotten the firearm six months ago – *where* the fuck he'd gotten it, she had no idea – probably one of his cronies – but he'd used up three bullets tonight that she knew of, which meant he had three left unless he was carrying spares.

Fuck.

That was three bullets too many.

She didn't know if Zane had ever killed anyone; she didn't get involved in what he did when he was out, or what he got up to, but he'd slowly started getting a little more pent up and unpredictable around the same time the gun had appeared. The way he'd pointed that thing at her tonight didn't seem like he'd never pulled that trigger on someone before.

Straining against the blackness, she searched out the cupboard for some kind of weapon.

"Where the fuck is she, you sack of shit."

No... Maybe Zane would hear her heart beating – god knew, she could barely make anything out above its hammering.

"You shot my hand earlier. She went to get help and locked the door behind her 'cause she was afraid you'd come back and finish me off. I don't know where she is now, but I'd be banking on the police getting here shortly if I were you."

No way he was going to fall for that bluff.

Something rattled and sloshed. The bedpan.

Zane cursed. "You. Get the fuck up and turn the lights on. Can't see a fucking thing."

"There's a switch by the wall, but it blew. The lights don't work."

"I said, get the fuck up!"

Oh, god... She heard shuffling.

After a while, Norman's voice came back with, "See? Fuse has gone."

Rosa's fingers closed around what felt like the wooden handle of a broom.

There was a muffled thump and then a low groan.

Rage festered inside her.

"Who are you? How do you know Rosa?"

This time, Norman's voice was strained. "I don't know her. I just met her tonight."

"Liar!"

"I'm not lying. Heard her scream in the alleyway – thought I'd be the good Samaritan."

Zane laughed. "You've got to be fucking kidding me."

Norman didn't reply.

There was silence, and then something that sounded like a gasp that she assumed came from Norman.

Her knuckles ached from gripping the broom. If Zane did anything to him, she'd kill him – as god was her witness, she'd *kill* him.

"Feel this gun against your skull?"

Fuck! No, no...

"I was aiming for Rosa's head last time 'cause she got me so angry I wasn't thinkin' straight. But she's a dumb whore who doesn't know any better. You did me a favour, 'cause I don't want my girl dead. You, on the other hand..." a whimper... "I couldn't give a toss about."

"NO!" The word tore from her lungs before she could stop it. She knew him – she knew Zane – and that tone he used was final. She slammed herself against the door. "Fuck you, Zane, you leave him the *fuck* alone!"

"Rosa?"

"POLICE!"

What?

"DROP YOUR WEAPON."

Everything fell silent at the unexpected command.

Feet marched into the room.

"Fucking *cunts*," she heard Zane toss out.

"DROP IT NOW."

A light beamed against the slats of the cupboard door...

"Go to hell."

...and then shot after shot rang out.

Chapter Nine

Screaming was the only thing that filled her mind – above all gunfire and yelling – her own voice piercing her ears, as she bulldozed into the door over and over again.

"NORMAN!"

There was so much goddamned *noise.*

"OPEN THE DOOR!"

She went at it with the broom, ramming its end against where she thought the lock was. Lights kept sweeping into the cupboard, broken by the slats. *Torches?*

Flinging the useless broom away, she threw herself at the door, and again, and again, and—

It flew open.

She went stumbling into arms, but not the ones she wanted. "Norman!"

"Miss…"

She wrenched herself free, scanning the room under the erratic streams of light, until her gaze landed on a head of brown hair, its owner unmoving on the floor.

"*Norman!*"

Her coat was grabbed. The buttons popped and she slipped right out of it until she was free of it, the force of her weight, no matter how slight, taking her where she needed to go.

"Hey!"

She ignored her protestor and landed squarely on Norman, and then *she* might as well have been shot – the stark realisation that speared through her was raw agony. With disbelief, she pulled herself back slowly, and drew her right hand up from where it had landed on his stomach. It was painted red.

Under his coat, which lay open, his shirt was soaked in blood.

Her gaze travelled up to his face.

Complexion, pasty.

Eyes closed.

Lips parted.

Still.

"NOOOOOOOOOOOO!"

It was an infinite caterwaul that ripped from her throat, and the room came alive. More people raced in, not all wearing police uniform. Arms grabbed at her, while she grabbed at him – *him* – Norman. *"Yes!"* she screamed, not even aware of what she was saying at this point. Thought had no place here anymore.

She was dragged back as green uniforms took over.

"Yes!" she cried again.

An oxygen mask went over his nose and mouth, head tipped back… "No pulse."

"I said, YES. Can't you fucking hear me!"

Chest compressions … one, two … but there was so much blood. It all seemed to pump out of him as they pumped his heart. "I need more pressure on the wound," one person said to another.

They complied … six, seven…

"I'll come with you! I'll stay with you!"

"Get her out of here."

"NO!" she struggled, but the hands on her were like vices.

"Jesus, we need her out. She's like a bloody ferret."

"We're calling this one," said someone else.

She whipped her head around in alarm.

The man who spoke knelt by Zane's head, and a bullet hole claimed the centre of it. For a second, she was dumbfounded and it ceased all her struggle. Zane was dead.

Zane's dead!

He'd been there for so long.

In her mind's eye, she saw herself march right to up him and spit on his body. In reality, she was still imprisoned by fists, trying to take her from...

"Norman," she whispered, turning back to him.

They were at it again. "...fourteen, fifteen." Air was pushed into his lungs using some kind of pump and tube that ran into the mask.

"I'll behave," she said, turning to look up at the officer who held her.

He shook his head. "You can't—"

"I'll keep still, I swear it. I won't get in the way. Please don't take me from him."

His eyes narrowed, but she didn't move an inch, and she had no idea why he listened – the police of all people – why *something* finally went her way, but he relaxed his grip on her a fraction, still searching out her eyes for any insincerity. "*One wrong move* and you're in a cell tonight – got it?"

"Yes. Thank you."

"...fourteen, fifteen. Again." Air was pumped.

Make it ... you have to make it.

Her blurry eyes, now used to the bright torch beams, caught a glint of something that lay between Zane and Norman.

Broken shards of porcelain. The doll-puppet had somehow got caught up in the frenzy and lay shattered on the floor, its cross flung metres from its body; its loose strings now with nothing to pull.

"...fourteen, fifteen." The paramedic pumped the air.

Norman's lungs rose with the pressure.

Norman's lungs fell.

Nothing else happened. No one moved.

Why have they stopped? Don't stop.

The one performing the compressions looked at the one holding the mask, solemnly.

Rosa shook her head, cold understanding washing over her, tears unstoppable. *No ... please no...*

"Call it."

~*~

The light was a warm glow, ridiculously bright, but not too bright to hurt, and not white like everyone said, but a golden yellow that sort of merged with skin so it was hard to see where you ended and it began.

Norman glanced at the odd image in front of him, right there on the grassy ground, in this abstract field that surrounded him. A strange kind of pride filled him at the great, hard-won accomplishment it represented. It didn't look like much if you didn't know everything it had taken to get to this point.

Fingers found those on his right hand and laced through them.

"You did it," he said, and turned to Rosa with a smile.

She, too, stared at the broken, life-sized doll on the ground. "I don't know how."

"It stopped mattering. In the very last second, this wasn't the most important thing, and now it never will be."

They both looked at the puppet, and before their eyes, all that was left of it disintegrated – porcelain, cotton, string ... until all that was left was the wooden cross.

She let go of his hand, walked forward and picked it up. Making her way back to him, she held out the cross for him to take, which he did, although a shiver of trepidation coursed through him at the feel of the wood in his palm.

Rising to her tiptoes, she pressed her lips against his. The light around them glowed brighter.

He didn't want it to end, but like all things, it did. "What's this for?" he asked, looking down at the cross.

"You decide," she whispered, a tear in her eye. "I can't make the choice for you."

And then she was fading, floating backwards as if on wheels, or flying through air. "Don't leave," he said. He wanted more time with her, and not to be left alone in this very bizarre place.

"Why did you do it?" she asked suddenly, before fading from sight.

"I told you why."

"Because of a vision? No ... really – why did you save me?"

The memory of that alleyway reformed in his mind, sharp and stark, Rosa pinned to the wall – way before he'd had the vision of her in that field. Before that, it hadn't been Rosa that had flashed through his mind, had it? It had been...

Tina in their bedroom, giving herself to another.

Him watching. Powerless.

"Because I could. Because what was happening wasn't your choice, and you could do nothing about it. But this time, I could. This time, I could change it."

She beamed him a smile. "So ... you saved yourself."

His own smile formed as the realisation sank in. "I guess I did."

"Good," she replied, her voice all but notes on the wind; her form no longer there. "Now, there's just one last choice to make."

A door stood where she had been, one solid object with no frame, in the middle of the landscape. It stood ajar. Erratic lights moved around in the dark at the other end – that was all he could see through the gap – and noise. Lots of noise, shouting, panicked voices, and one above all others... "I said, YES. Can't you fucking hear me!"

His heart leapt in his chest – literally. Like someone had it in their hands and was squeezing it, thumping it. He dropped the cross, startled.

It clattered on the ground, and he frowned, wondering how it could make that sound on grass, only when he looked down, he saw himself standing at the centre of a cemented crossroad that had paved itself through the field.

At the far end of the crossroad, opposite the door, there was a channel of light reaching from sky to ground – beautiful, strong, unbroken – promising eternity. It looked good ... by god, that looked good. He walked towards it, but stopped in his tracks when he spied a scene from the past on the path leading west.

Tina giving birth to their first child.

He teared up; took a step that way instead.

She looked up at him and smiled, now holding their precious bundle in her arms. "I hurt," she said through her smile, tears streaming down her face. "I hurt so much – it was so painful, but look..." She held up their beautiful daughter. "It was so, so worth it."

Something slammed into his chest.

He groaned, and gritted his teeth as he doubled over in pain. "Fuck," he gasped out.

"Son..."

"What...?" He looked east. All pain became temporarily forgotten as he set eyes on his father. A new kind of hurt bloomed. Nearly thirty years... "Dad," he said, the single syllable breaking.

"What the fuck you doing here, boy?" His Welsh cadence both warmed him and pierced him – he never thought he'd hear that voice again. "You're wasting time."

"Dad," he said again, feeling a little stupid, because it was all he could think to say, and it was just nice to keep saying it – to call him 'Dad' – to be able to call out to his dad after all this time.

"You need to make a decision."

"I can't. I..." Pain speared though his chest again, making him gasp. "Jesus," he cried, vision blurring, "It hurts."

"Everything that matters hurts, until it doesn't matter anymore."

He looked west again, at Tina holding Lindsey, only now, the scene had changed and Lindsey was eight, holding her five-year-old sister's hand as she helped her onto a sled, the snow thick around them.

What had he lost? He'd lost his entire world.

And just like that he started to sob for the first time – crumpled into a ball of mess. He finally knew it was over. Hope – or perhaps delusion – was a flame that had stayed lit, even though its scorching light would hurt. It had refused to go out. Somewhere inside him, he'd been adamant that he would take Tina back; he could make it work, would make it work ... but something had changed.

In that alleyway.

That was the moment.

That was when the shift had happened and he'd known without a doubt, it could never go back to the way it had been – he could never go back – even if she apologised and returned with open arms, speaking promises of forever. He had changed. And he had no idea what happened next; what the new way was.

"Ten ... nine ... eight..."

He looked up, bewildered, at his dad's counting down.

"What's going on?"

"Time's up, son."

A gunshot rang out, blasting through the light that surrounded the field, only he couldn't see it – couldn't tell where the hell it had come from.

"Norman..." His name – a whisper floating on the air, through the gap in the door... Rosa...

The bullet would hit him if he didn't fucking move, but which way to go? He looked away from the door, back at the channel of light. It would wash all pain away, he was certain of that.

"...five ... four ... three..."

I don't know what we're doing here – you and me ... I don't know what we are or what we can be, but this doesn't have to be about that. This can just be about ... a chance. Taking a chance.

His own words.

Not for her – for him.

"...two..."

He ran.

Have to make it... *'Cause whichever way he went there was no going back, and he didn't want to die. He wasn't ready – not yet – even if everything hurt like hell. It mattered that things mattered.*

Too late!

Was he too late?

Where there had been lights and noise and chaos and shouting, all was now silent.

Not too late ... please, not too late! *He curled his fingers around the door...*

"...one..."

"Call it."

...and pushed.

~*~

She was trying to hold it together. Even so, her crying was the only sound in the room.

The paramedic holding the mask released it, and pulled it off him.

God ... this hurt ... too much. More than bruises. More than anything Zane had ever done to her.

The policeman behind her let out a quiet sigh.

The paramedic looked down at his wristwatch. "Time of death, five-oh—"

Norman gasped.

Every single person froze, not sure they'd heard or seen what they'd seen. Or maybe they believed it was the body simply relaxing. She'd read that that happened sometimes – that muscles could contract, even after death.

Norman choked, coughing, trying to clear his—

"Jesus Christ! Dopamine 5 mcg – now. Keep the pressure on this wound – get the trolley!" Needles went in veins, drips were hooked up, someone wheeled in a bed; all three paramedics went to work on him, and Rosa was having trouble breathing herself.

"Rosa!"

Someone was calling her name. She felt her head move towards one of the paramedics. "You Rosa?"

"*Rosa...*" Her eyes widened as her name slipped from Norman's lips, barely audible. She nodded.

"Get over here."

The policeman prodded her from behind, "Go." And

suddenly, everything fell into place, became three-dimensional, and came alive.

Alive! "Norman..." She stumbled towards him, not able to feel her legs at all.

One of the paramedics steadied her, brought her over, and placed her by his side. "Stay in this spot, so we can work around you." And then she was touching him, her hand slipping into his right.

His eyes flickered open briefly. "Rosa..." he whispered again.

"Here. I'm right here."

He smiled, and she felt the wall around her heart crack as joy ran her through – real joy – the likes of which she'd never known before. She found herself thanking god, or whoever the powers that be were – probably the first time she ever had.

"I made it," he uttered, his voice breaking with hoarseness.

His eyes closed as he slipped from consciousness.

She reached up and stroked his hair. "We both made it."

Chapter Ten

It was strangely comforting – the beeps and murmurs from the people around him, the quiet conversations and the occasional presence of someone near.

He didn't know who they were, but he always knew when it was Rosa, not because he heard her voice – although sometimes he managed to catch the tail end of something she was saying – but because he felt her warmth and it seeped into him. He felt warm when she was near, and now, x-amount of time on, consciousness prodded him, awareness no longer willing to fade, but bringing him to the present and the reality that awaited him.

Coming to was painful.

His body ached; his head ached; his heart ached. His left hand throbbed heavy and dull, and his left side, around his stomach, was definitely not as it should be. However, the sharp edge of all the pain, in itself, seemed blunt – dampened.

Morphine, answered his mind, before he could fully form the question.

He opened his eyes to lights too bright, and let out a small sound of protest.

A chair screeched across the floor, far too loudly to his ears, and then warmth cascaded down on him – *her* warmth. "Norman?"

His eyes followed the sound of his name, and he gave what he hoped was a smile, as intended.

She beamed at him. No – she radiated.

Beautiful.

She reached up to stroke his hair, and he let out a sigh. *Don't ever stop.* Her touch felt like the chalice of life. "How long...?" he tried to say, although his voice seemed not to be working so well.

"It's been four days. Today's December 10th. You're doing well. You lost a lot of blood – we thought we lost you completely at first." Her blue eyes filled with tears. The bruising on her cheek looked so much better – stark and painful, but better. "But you came back," she smiled. "You've been stable since, but ... there was some damage to your left kidney. Thankfully, nothing irreparable, although they're not yet sure whether it'll fully function or not. But you're doing great. Really great." She took his right hand in hers. "I've missed you."

"You've ... been here ... every day." Fuck. Talking was hard.

She stared at him, surprised. "Yeah ... you knew?"

"Can ... hear."

"Oh."

"Missed you ... too."

She smiled again, although this time, there was a hint of sadness to it.

He didn't want that – no more sadness. "Zane?"

"Dead," she said.

He let out a grunt, but stopped short of saying, *Good.* Perhaps that was too callous. Finding happiness in another's demise was not a trait he wanted, but he couldn't deny his sense of relief, not just for him, but for her.

"I've given the police a statement. They'll want one

from you when you're able, but I don't think there's any rush. It was the police that shot him. And he shot you – reflex action, they said." Rosa bent down and gave his hand a kiss.

He wanted that kiss on his lips.

She reached over him to his bedside table and picked up a small plastic bag. "Before we left that building, I grabbed my coat, and your stuff." He spied his wallet in the bag, along with his wedding ring, sitting right there in the very corner of the bottom of the bag.

She placed it back. "You've had a few visitors. I've, um … I've kept out of the way when they're here. They've seen me a couple of times, but don't know who I am." She looked nervous.

He was confused for all of two seconds until he finally caught on.

Jesus … she didn't have to worry about that. It was over. Finally. She'd been his epiphany.

He wished he could move – touch her face – and that's when he noticed something different about her. *Bit slow today, aren't you, Norman?*

He told snarky Norman to shut the fuck up. He'd been on the brink of death – twice – and he didn't need *that* Norman in his head anymore. "Your hair…"

"Oh," her hand flew up to her head. Her face went red.

Her gorgeous blonde hair hung down in soft waves to just above her shoulders, about a third shorter, and her dreadlocks were gone.

"There was … um … there was blood on it, and … you know, it feels kinda nice this way. I forgot how heavy all those dreads were," she laughed.

"You look beautiful."

Her face heated up again as another smile lit it.

He *had* to kiss her. "Rosa..."

"*Daddy!*"

His hand was dropped.

"Oh, my god, Dad..." Two blonde bundles came at him, thankfully mindful of all his injuries. He was engulfed in half-hugs and kisses. He smelt their shampoo in their hair, and underlying that, their signature scents he'd known from birth – his Lindsey; his Gemma... Tears choked him. "My girls." It was so bloody good to see them.

And then, everyone was sobbing.

Tina's tear-streaked face came into view above him. She could barely hold a smile for crying.

"All right, people, some space, please." A female doctor marched into his line of vision and parted them all with her efficiency. "Good to see you awake, Mr Smithson. If you can spare ten minutes from your family, I could do with checking you over – make sure everything's working as it should."

"Girls," said Tina, her voice thick, "come on. Let's wait outside."

"Thank you. I'll call you in as soon as I'm done."

"Thank you, doctor."

Tina placed a kiss on his forehead. "I'm so glad you're back," she whispered.

And he had no idea what to say.

It was good to see her – it was – but faint anger towards her still existed, as well as a refreshing acceptance. He'd moved on since he'd last spoken to her.

He finally settled on, "Me, too." It was the truth – he was glad to be back.

As they retreated from the room, he scanned everywhere he could for Rosa.

She was gone.

~*~

"Here ... I've got it." said Tina, flapping around him for the hundredth time. He sighed and bit his tongue. He was grateful for the help – unfortunately, he could do with it – but really wished he didn't need it. Time on his own, after the restrictions of the hospital, would be gold. Having Rosa here would be even better, but he tried to push her out of his mind.

He hadn't seen her since that first time he'd opened his eyes two weeks ago. It cut him, and he didn't know what it meant.

Zane was dead now. She could carry on without him. Perhaps that Dan bloke was looking after her.

His gut churned thinking about it, right along with an irrepressible longing. *She needs to be here.*

But he had to respect her wishes, and she clearly wanted to stay away. It's not like they knew each other. They'd spent one night together and it had been a night fraught with pain and danger – those weren't things he wanted to represent to her.

She's better off without you – let her start anew.

Tina shut the door behind him, and he surveyed his little bedsit, exactly as he'd left it before he'd gone out to the pub that fateful night.

"I wish you'd change your mind and come and stay at the house. It's still your home, you know. And look at this place ... it's Christmas Eve and you don't even have a tree."

"I don't want to stay at the house, Tina."

She stared at him, nibbled on her lip, and then shrugged her shoulders. "Let me make us tea."

"All right – thanks. I'd show you where the kitchen is,

but it begins there, and ends there."

She laughed even though she tried not to.

He smiled.

Tina's busyness was comforting – familiar. She'd been her usual strong, mothering self after he'd woken up, and he hadn't wanted for anything.

Except Rosa.

He sat himself down at the two-seater table in the room and tried to relax; averted his eyes from the cast that covered his left wrist and hand. He'd spend tomorrow at the house with Tina and the kids. Tina had insisted, and he wasn't going to say no – not on Christmas Day. Part of him was looking forward to it.

Part of him felt empty.

He reasoned it was the shock of it all, and the change from hospital to home. There was also the looming future. The doctors all said he should be okay for travel in March, as long as he took it easy. And the bones in his hand should be mostly healed by then. Taking it easy wasn't a problem with no job and, right now, he was grateful he didn't have one. Worrying about work while trying to heal would have sent his stress levels rocketing.

Tina brought two cups of tea over and sat down. "How do you feel being back ... here."

He glanced at her, almost laughing. She really didn't like the bedsit. Tina had always preferred the finer things in life. "I don't feel much of anything yet. I guess it'll take a few days for it all to sink in."

She nodded and they both sipped their drinks.

"I'm worried about you here on your own. Who's going to help you if you need—"

"I'll be fine," he assured her.

"Maybe, but..." She took a deep breath, and he knew

what was coming; had sensed her working up to this over the past two weeks in the little things she did and said. "I was so horrible." She welled up. "What I did to you ... it wasn't me; I wasn't thinking straight."

"Tina—"

"After I got the call saying you'd been shot," her face fell and she began to cry. "I ended it with Chad. I made such a bad mistake, and I don't know if you can ever forgive me, but ... please consider coming home. I *do* still love you. Almost losing you the way I did, I ... I was an idiot, Norman, and I didn't realise what I had – what *we* had. I want us to try again. For us, for the kids... I swear, I'll never hurt you again – not like that."

She stared at him, all hopeful, and then finally ducked her head when she got no reaction.

In truth, he was waiting for a reaction himself. Just a month ago, her words would have been heaven. They would have been everything he'd been longing to hear, but now...

"Tina ... I've changed."

"I know," she looked up, earnestly. "You've been to hell and back, and some crazy person shot you, and—"

"No. I mean I've changed *inside*."

She held his gaze, clearly trying to understand what he meant. How did you put into words something not solid?

"It tore me up, catching you with him, like *that*."

"I know," she wailed, "I'm so, so—"

"Don't. Saying sorry is kind of irrelevant. Saying sorry doesn't make it any better – it still happened. For six months."

She stopped talking – sobbed quietly instead.

"You're not the only one who sacrificed things over the past twenty years, you know? There's so little I've done for *me* in that time. And I was okay with it. I mean, the girls are worth it – they're worth it all. You were worth it.

"That night I got shot ... it's really hard to explain, but I did something for myself that night – for *me*. I didn't realise it at the time."

"I'm still not a hundred percent clear on what happened. You haven't really talked about it."

"I heard a girl getting hit in an alleyway – more than hit." Anger surfaced once more at that image. He had to put a lid on it. "I thought about turning away, but I couldn't, and then I saw Rosa, and them, and what they were doing to her, and ... I stepped in."

"Jesus, Norman..."

"At the time, I thought I'd done it for her, and I guess I sort of did, but ... later, I realised it had been for me, too. I lost everything when I lost you." He couldn't help it – his voice caught, tears forming in his eyes. "And I couldn't stop it – I couldn't stop what I saw in our bedroom, but I could stop what was happening in that alleyway. I could stop her losing everything, too. In that moment, I changed. I stood up for myself. And in doing so, I accepted it – losing you. And I can't take that away now. I don't want to. I can't go back."

A stunned silence ensued.

He took another sip of tea.

She looked bewildered.

Another sip.

"Was that her? At the hospital? There was a blonde girl ... I saw her a couple of times in your room – thought she was the nurse at first until I realised she wasn't wearing a uniform. Bruise on her cheek. She never stopped to say anything – scooted out of there whenever I came by, like a scared rabbit."

His heart twinged at his loss of her, too. "Yes. That was Rosa."

He said nothing else, after all, what would be the point? He didn't know if he and Rosa were anything beyond what had happened that night. Telling Tina about it would only hurt her, and no matter what she'd done to him, he didn't want to cause her pain unnecessarily.

She knew him well though – always had. She studied his face, then said, quietly, no lack of disapproval in her tone, "She's half your age."

Thank god for tea. He used it to stop his retort coming out: *She's older than she looks.* It was none of her business, and bringing Rosa into this didn't seem right. He had nothing to justify to Tina.

She sighed. "Look ... you've been through so much. You're bound to feel confused. You don't need to make a decision now. We can wait until the New Year and then—"

"I'm going away in March."

That certainly shut her up, although he hated the crestfallen look on her face. "Away? Where?"

"Kenya. For six months initially. It's paid work and training at a safari park and sanctuary. You know I've always wanted to work with animals."

It didn't seem like she could form words. "That's ... that's ... that's crazy. At your age?"

Annoyance raced up his spine. "I'm going, Tina. I want to."

"But you're injured."

"I'll be mostly healed by then."

"But—"

"I'm *going*, Tina."

She sat back in her chair, dumbfounded. "The kids..."

He deflated within, feeling the cost of it all. "I'll miss them enormously, and I know they'll miss me, but I need to work, and that work has to be something I really want to do with my life. At least, it *should* be, if it can be."

She gave her head a shake, maybe to help the information sink in. "Okay. Okay ... that's ... if that's what you want, I'm happy for you. I am. It'll give you time to think being away from it all, and when you come back, maybe we can—"

"No, Tina."

She looked up at him, eyes filling with tears anew at the finality in his tone. "No?"

He shook his head, sadly. "No."

Tina let herself out, right after they'd made concrete the plans for tomorrow. It was a bittersweet goodbye in some ways, without goodbye actually being said. But it was also a weight off his entire being. Now, he could move forward, wherever that led.

With his body protesting, he stood and made his way to the radio in the kitchen, needing some form of sound to drown out the quiet he still wasn't used to after the bustle of the hospital.

It flashed through his mind that he should go back to the pub in Whitechapel and see if he could speak to Rosa through Dan. Three things stopped him: he wasn't ready to face that place again, not so soon; the journey there would probably be the end of him as he was still pretty battered (he really didn't want to rupture his kidney all over again), and Rosa had chosen to stay away.

No matter how he felt about that, he refused to be the

one to take that choice away from a person who had never had choice in her life in the first place.

He flicked the radio to ON.

...Love's young dream, alas, is over,
Yet my strains of love shall hover
Near the presence of my lover
All through the night...

Grunting, and unamused, he went to find another channel when the buzzer sounded. He automatically scanned the room to see what Tina had left behind as he made his way to the front door, the pain in his left side still 'causing him to limp. Thank god he'd chosen a bedsit on the ground floor, 'cause there was no elevator in this building, and walking to the top floor would have been agony.

He swung his door open and...

Don't fall over, Norman.

"Hi," said Rosa.

Oh, my god... He couldn't speak. He'd resigned himself to the fact he was never going to bloody see her again.

Say things, Norman.

All at once, she looked uncertain. "Um ... if this is a bad time..."

He tried. He honestly tried, but nothing came out, and she was so fucking gorgeous standing there with her woolly hat over the waves of her hair and framing her big, sky-blue eyes, her bruise all but gone... His angel. No longer fallen.

Her cheeks went red. "I waited, um, until your wife left. I know I haven't been to see you, but," she took in a shaky breath, "I wanted to give you time ... with them. I wanted to come – I really did – but ... you know ... it's

Christmas, and ... your family is..." Her voice trailed off, and her eyes welled up.

He looked down and saw a big rucksack by her feet, and a waist-high rectangular box to her right. She'd carried those all the way here, battling people on the tube trains, on Christmas Eve?

"Your address was in your wallet, on your driver's licence, and I made note of it before I gave it back. And I *totally* understand if you've changed your mind."

Changed my mind?

"I almost didn't come ... I wasn't sure, and it's not like your phone number was in your wallet ... but anyway, I did stop by to check on your place earlier in the week – just to make sure it was okay. I mean, obviously, I don't have a key, but I peeped through the window to make sure everything looked all right. Figured you wouldn't have had anyone know to do that for you – don't think the neighbours liked my peeping much, by the way," she let out a small laugh as a tear fell down her cheek of its own accord.

She was babbling.

She was *real*.

And she was standing right in front of him.

"Anyway, I couldn't see a Christmas tree and this one's a spare from mine." Her hand landed on the box. "It comes with lights and everything, and I don't mind helping you put it up and we can switch the lights on together later. *Even* if you've changed your mind. I mean, we're friends, right? And I would understand if you decided you wanted to try again after everything that's happened. I mean, with your wife."

Oh, hell no.

He finally moved, ignoring all his aches, and stepped right out that door, took her face in his one working hand

and did exactly what he'd been longing to do since he'd first seen her watching over him, just like his angel would, in the hospital.

Her lips parted just before his met hers, a soft sigh escaping them, and it was the breath of life for him. It was a shot in the dark. It was a chance he wanted to take.

The tip of his tongue gently stroked hers, and her slender arms came up around his waist, not pressing too hard.

He didn't want to pull back, but he did want to look at her face again.

Her eyes remained closed for a few seconds after the kiss ended. They shone when she opened them. "So ... you still want me to come stay with you?"

He wiped her tear away. "I said, yes. Can't you fucking hear me?"

Her eyes widened in shock and she let out a sharp breath. "Norman..." More tears slipped down as she fell into his chest.

He cradled her there, sending out a silent 'thank you' that she came back.

"You heard me? I can't believe you heard me." Her voice shook.

"Loud and clear," he said, his own voice thick. "I thought you'd changed *your* mind."

"No ... fuck, no."

"Thank god. Is this your stuff in your rucksack?"

"Pretty much all of it. I don't have a lot."

He went to pick it up, but she stopped him. "Oh, no you don't. No lifting. I've got it. Carried these all the way here myself."

"Okay then," he held his door open. "Come in," he smiled. "Kettle's full, heating's on, lights are on, radio's on..."

...Earthly dust from off thee shaken,
Soul immortal shalt thou awaken...

She hesitated for a second, looking a little overwhelmed as she contemplated the next step.

With thy last dim journey taken...

Then, she smiled back at him, walked into his home – *her* new home – and he shut the door behind them.

...home through the night.

The End

Acknowledgements / Author's Note

I feel like I repeat myself every time with acknowledgements, but the usual key people step up every time to make publishing on time possible and a pleasure. Ninfa Hayes, Elizabeth Morgan, Amanda L. Pederick (aka The Picky Bitch), Hot Tree Promotions, my ARC readers and a number of dedicated bloggers, my Street Team, and certainly not least, my partner, Alastair, who deals with the fall out as I 'become' these characters that I write.

Broken Lights was an impromptu idea that came out of nowhere and I desperately wanted to get it down. I hope you enjoyed reading it as much as I enjoyed writing it.

Dianna Hardy
7th December, 2014

Also by Dianna Hardy

The Witching Pen series
And the companion novel, *Saving Eve.*

Witches, angels, demons, Heaven and Hell all come together in a dizzying story of friendship, love and forgiveness. A titillating mix of paranormal romance and urban fantasy brings you a sensational series you won't forget.

Eye of the Storm series
This international bestselling fantasy series is now complete. Werewolves living in the Surrey Hills come face to face with family secrets, ancient mythology, and monsters – both human and created – that want them extinct. Humorous and highly erotic in places, this is dark paranormal fantasy, not for the faint of heart.

Blood Never Lies (Duet)
Two companion novels to the *Eye of the Storm* series that also stand on their own and act as prequels to a brand new series each. Dark Urban Fantasy.

Once Times Thrice series
Practical Magic meets Serendipity in a beautiful, fun, and magical series about love, family, and second chances, set in Cornwall, England. Follow Merri, Jamie, Pippa, Jimmy and Candy as summer turns to autumn. Contemporary romance with a touch of magic.

'Til Death Do Us Part
(an Adult Retelling of The Little Mermaid)
An adult fairy tale novelette. In this dark and passionate retelling of The Little Mermaid, can a love founded on humanity stand the passing of time, an angry sea-God, and even death itself?

A Silver Kiss (Vampire Poetry)
A dark and daring addition to the literary world of vampirism, this is a collection of rhyming and freestyle poetry that explores the often taboo themes of power, possession and seduction.

Emotionally charging, each poem is written from a different perspective, be it the hunter or the hunted and inspires a deeper look into the psychology of the human mind and the darker aspects of human relationships and society.

All books can be viewed at
diannahardy.com

About the Author

Dianna Hardy is the international bestselling author of
The Witching Pen series and the *Eye Of The Storm series.*
She writes (often cross-genre) fantasy fiction, combining
anything from paranormal romance to horror, to creation
myths and god-punk, as well as a healthy dose of the
erotic into her writing. Her stories are action-packed, and
fast-paced, with a focus on both character development
and the plot.

She currently lives in South Hampshire, UK with her
partner and their daughter, where she writes full-time.

Website: diannahardy.com
Email: dianna@diannahardy.com

Facebook: facebook.com/authordiannahardy
Twitter: twitter.com/thewitchingpen
Instagram: instagram/diannahardy.author